ROBOT to the RESCUE

by Kay Lawrence
illustrated by Sergio de Giorgi

Kane Press
New York

For Dad and Grandpa U.
—K.L.

To Abril, Emma, and Vivi, with love
—S.D.G.

Library of Congress Cataloging-in-Publication Data
Names: Lawrence, Kay, author. | De Giorgi, Sergio, illustrator.
Title: Robot to the rescue / by Kay Lawrence ; illustrated by Sergio de Giorgi.
Description: New York : Kane Press, 2018. | Series: Makers make it work |
Summary: Greta wants to go on an overnight trip with her mother and her friend, but first she must find a way to make their plant-watering robot feed the cat while they are away.
Identifiers: LCCN 2017020314 (print) | LCCN 2017036878 (ebook) |
ISBN 9781575659886 (ebook) | ISBN 9781575659879 (pbk) | ISBN 9781635920116 (reinforced library binding)
Subjects: | CYAC: Robots—Fiction. | Robotics—Fiction. | Cats—Fiction.
Classification: LCC PZ7.1.L3887 (ebook) | LCC PZ7.1.L3887 Rob 2018 (print) |
DDC [E]—dc23
LC record available at https://lccn.loc.gov/2017020314

10 9 8 7 6 5 4 3 2 1

First published in the United States of America in 2018 by Kane Press, Inc.
Printed in China

Makers Make It Work is a trademark of Kane Press, Inc.

Book Design: Michelle Martinez

Visit us online at **www.kanepress.com**

 Like us on Facebook
facebook.com/kanepress

Greta stood in her kitchen next to a robot. The robot had two wheels, one long arm with a gripper . . . and a loose screw.

"I'll fix that!" Greta said. She picked up a screwdriver to tighten the screw. Then she heard a knock at the door.

"Hi, Bruce! Come in and meet Water-Bot!"
Greta said. "Mom and I built it. It waters our
plants. Watch!"

She picked up a cell phone from the counter and touched the screen. Water-Bot began to move.

Greta's cat, Freddy, hissed and jumped up onto the fridge. "Sorry, Freddy," Greta called. "Freddy hates Water-Bot," she told Bruce.

Water-Bot rolled to the counter. It grabbed a watering can in its gripper. Greta touched the screen again. Water-Bot turned. It rolled over to a potted plant and tilted the can down. Water poured onto the plant.

Robots come in all shapes and sizes. They can be smaller than a grain of rice or longer than a school bus!

"Cool! Can I try?" Bruce asked.

"Sure!" Greta handed him the phone.

Bruce made Water-Bot spin around. "This is awesome!" he said.

Greta's mom came in. "I see Bruce has met our new friend," she said.

"Oh!" Bruce said. "I almost forgot why I came over! It snowed in the mountains. Mom and I are going to spend the night in our cabin. Do you guys want to come?"

"Can we, Mom?" Greta bounced up and down with excitement. Suddenly she froze. "Wait—we can't. Who would take care of Freddy? We've never left him alone at night before."

"Can't you leave his food out?" Bruce asked.

"He'd eat it all the minute we left," Greta said. "Then he'd be hungry all night." She sighed.

Water-Bot gently bumped into Greta.

"Oops! Sorry," said Bruce. He touched the screen and Water-Bot backed up.

"Hey!" said Greta. "Maybe *Water-Bot* can feed Freddy!"

The word "robot" comes from the Czech word "robota," which means "forced labor."

"That's a good idea," Greta's mom said. She looked at the clock. "But I have work to finish. If you figure it out, we can go."

"Yes!" Greta and Bruce high-fived.

Greta pulled out pencils and paper. Then she and Bruce sat down at the table.

"How can Water-Bot feed Freddy?" Greta asked. Bruce tapped his pencil on the table. Greta doodled on the paper.

"I know!" Bruce jumped to his feet. "Let's put a plastic cup of food on the edge of the table. Then we crash Water-Bot into the table. *Blam!* The food will fall onto the floor!"

"But Mom likes this table," Greta said. "She wouldn't want Water-Bot crashing into it."

Greta doodled some more. Bruce tapped
some more.

"Maybe . . ." Greta frowned, thinking hard.
"Oh! Maybe Water-Bot can pour cat food
instead of water!"

"Yes!" Bruce said.

Greta emptied the watering can and dried the inside. She poured cat kibble into the can and tilted it.

"Nope." Greta shook her head. "The spout is too small."

"We could use this," said Bruce. He picked up a cup.

"Good idea!" Greta said. She filled the cup with kibble and put the cup in Water-Bot's gripper. Then she made the gripper twist.

Only a few bits of kibble fell out.

"The cup needs to tilt more. Then all the kibble will fall out," said Greta.

Greta grabbed a piece of paper. "Right now the gripper twists this far." She drew an arrow showing how far the gripper twisted.

"And we need it to twist this far." Bruce drew another picture beside it.

Greta used a wrench to loosen a bolt. She pulled on Water-Bot's gripper. It popped off in her hand.

She put it back in at a different angle and tightened the bolt again.

Bruce put food into the cup. Greta made the gripper twist. Kibble fell into the bowl.

"Woo-hoo!" said Bruce. He patted the robot on its head. "You're not Water-Bot anymore. You're Kibble-Bot!"

FREDDY

The first robot may have been a mechanical bird made in Greece around 350 BCE.

"What if something goes wrong? I wish we could see Kibble-Bot feed Freddy," Greta said, scratching Freddy's back. "Hey! I know!"

She raced out of the room. She came back with a little camera. "We can put this on Kibble-Bot's head! The camera is linked to Mom's phone. That way we can watch the kitchen while we're gone!"

Bruce handed Greta long pieces of tape.
Greta taped the camera to Kibble-Bot's head.

Greta's mom walked in just as they were finishing. "Wow! Good work!" she said. "I guess we'd better pack our snow clothes!"

Greta ran upstairs, her heart thumping. She packed boots, gloves, a warm coat, and a hat.

Today robots are used to
build things, fight fires,
even explore other planets!

Before she left, she filled Kibble-Bot's cup
with cat food. She turned on the camera.
Then she gave Freddy a hug good-bye.
"Take good care of him, Kibble-Bot," she said.

At the cabin,
Greta and Bruce had
a snowball fight.

They built snow people. They built a snow
robot.

"Ready for cocoa?" Ms. Ling called from the
cabin door.

"Yes!" Greta and Bruce yelled.

They drank cocoa and had dinner. Afterward
Greta picked up her mom's phone. "Time to feed
Freddy!" she said.

She turned on the camera. Everyone gathered around the phone. Greta could see Kibble-Bot's gripper holding the food.

"Here goes," said Greta.

She moved Kibble-Bot over to the food bowl. She pressed the arm control. Kibble-Bot's gripper tilted. The kibble spilled into the bowl.

"Hooray!" said Bruce.

"But where's Freddy?"
Greta asked.

Greta spun Kibble-Bot
around slowly. Freddy wasn't
on the fridge.

He wasn't on
the high shelf. He
wasn't behind the
cookbooks.

"Those are all his usual hiding spots," Greta said,
frowning.

"Don't worry," said her mom. "Once Kibble-Bot
stops moving, Freddy will come out to eat."

Before bedtime, Greta checked the camera again. Sure enough, the bowl was empty. But she couldn't see Freddy anywhere.

"Maybe he's hiding somewhere new," said Bruce.

Greta bit her lip. "He must be upset that we're gone. Poor Freddy!"

In the morning, there was still no sign of Freddy. They packed up the car. "I'm worried about Freddy," Greta said.

"I'm sure he's fine," said Ms. Ling, "but worrying is no fun."

The trip seemed to take forever. When they got home, Greta jumped out of the car. "Hurry, Mom!" she said.

Greta's mom unlocked the door. The door swung open. Greta ran into the kitchen and . . .

There was Freddy! Greta blinked. She couldn't believe it. Freddy was curled up on Kibble-Bot's base! He looked up at her and meowed.

Bruce laughed. "That's why we couldn't find him with the camera. He was in the one spot the camera couldn't see."

"Freddy and Kibble-Bot are friends now!" Greta said.

"Cats like whoever feeds them," her mom said.

"Speaking of food, who wants lunch?" asked
Greta's mom.

"Me!" said Greta.

"Me!" said Bruce.

"Me!" said Ms. Ling.

"Meow!" said Freddy.

Learn Like a Maker

Have you heard the phrase, "If at first you don't succeed, try, try again"? Greta and Bruce succeeded in turning Water-Bot into Kibble-Bot, but it took a few tries to get it just right. Inventors know things don't always work perfectly the first time you try them!

Look Back

- Look at pages 15–16. What challenges did Greta and Bruce have? How did they handle the challenges?

- On pages 20–21, they added a camera to Kibble-Bot to improve it even more. What is something else they could have done to their robot to improve it?

Try This!

Change Maker
Look around your home or school for something you can change and make better. (Make sure you get an adult's permission before making any changes!)

- First, what does the item do now?

- Next, what would you like it to do?

- Brainstorm ways you can change the item. What will you need to make the change?

Try making the change. Did it work the first time? If it didn't, don't give up! What else can you try to make it work?

Food Photography:
From
Snapshots to
Great Shots

Second Edition

Nicole S. Young

Peachpit
Press

Food Photography: From Snapshots to Great Shots
Second Edition
Nicole S. Young

Peachpit Press
www.peachpit.com

To report errors, please send a note to errata@peachpit.com
Peachpit Press is a division of Pearson Education.

Project Editor: Valerie Witte
Production Editor: Tracey Croom
Copy Editor: Linda Laflamme
Proofreader: Kim Wimpsett
Composition: Danielle Foster
Indexer: James Minkin
Cover Image: Nicole S. Young
Cover Design: Aren Straiger
Interior Design: Mimi Heft
Author Photo: Dav.d Daniels

ISBN-13: 978-0-134-09713-8
ISBN-10: 0-134-09713-0

9 8 7 6 5 4 3 2 1
Printed and bound in the United States of America

Dedication

To my husband, Brian, for being my best friend, partner, and all-time favorite person. Thank you for your love, for your support, and for being my personal cheerleader… as well as for your patience while I photograph the food before we eat it. I love you!

Acknowledgments

Creating a book is no small task. The process of writing, editing, and publishing a book is, at times, overwhelming. It's a creative challenge to make the content work within the pages; teach the reader (as clearly as possible) about technique, skill, vision, and creativity; and also stay true to the layout, flow, and structure of the book itself. My name may be on the cover of the book, but I'm really only a part of the process, and there's no way that this book would be what it is without the guidance, hard work, dedication, inspiration, and motivation of so many other people.

I wouldn't be where I am today without the support and love from my family. They believe in me (and always have) and never doubt my ability to succeed at whatever I set my mind and heart to do, and because of that, I will be forever grateful. I love you guys!

I am blessed with an amazing group of friends, mentors, and colleagues. You all have opened my eyes to things I couldn't see without your guidance, and you have also been the voice of reason when I stumbled. Thank you for your never-ending dedication, loyalty, and patience. Thank you also for your wisdom, advice, and knowledge, and, even more importantly, thank you for giving me hope and inspiring confidence.

I want to thank the Peachpit crew and the team involved in producing this book, especially my editors, Linda and Valerie. Thank you for your patience, flexibility, and teamwork while working on this book.

I am extremely thankful to my readers. It means so much to me when I get a note from someone thanking me for a book, a blog post, or a bit of knowledge that helped him or her become a better photographer. You, my readers, are the reason I wrote this book, and I, in turn, have learned so much from being part of an amazing, worldwide, kind, and generous community of creative and talented people.

Contents

INTRODUCTION   X

CHAPTER 1: FOOD PHOTOGRAPHY FUNDAMENTALS   3

The Tools and Setup for Digital Food Photography

Poring Over the Picture   4
Poring Over the Picture   6
Digital Cameras   8
  The Limitations of the P&S   8
  DSLR and Mirrorless   11
  Full-Frame versus Crop Sensor   12
  Which Camera Should I Buy?   14
Lenses and Focal Lengths   15
  Wide-Angle   15
  Midrange   16
  Telephoto   17
  Macro Lenses   17
Tripods and Accessories   21
  Tripods and Camera Stands   21
  Tripod Heads   21
  Cable Releases   22
Working with Digital Files   23
  RAW vs. JPEG   23
  White Balance   24
The Exposure Triangle: Aperture, Shutter Speed, and ISO   26
  Aperture   27
  Shutter Speed   27
  ISO   30
  Calculating Overall Exposure   32
Chapter 1 Challenges   35

CHAPTER 2: LIGHTING   37

Techniques and Equipment for Lighting Food

Poring Over the Picture   38
Poring Over the Picture   40
Types of Light   42
  Natural Light   42
  Artificial Light   42

Lighting Modifiers and Accessories   46
    Reflectors   46
    Diffusers   47
Quality of Light   48
    Color   49
    Intensity   50
    Distance   50
Direction of Light   51
    Backlight   51
    Sidelight   53
    Frontlight   56
Chapter 2 Challenges   59

CHAPTER 3: STYLING AND PROPS   **61**

The Art of Presentation
Poring Over the Picture   62
Poring Over the Picture   64
Styling Considerations   66
    Using a Food Stylist   66
    Ethical Considerations   66
    Styled Food vs. Real Food   67
Ensuring Food Quality   69
    Using Fresh Ingredients   69
    Shopping Smartly   69
Food Styling Basics   71
    Gadgets and Tools   71
    Using Stand-ins   72
    Maintaining a Clean Environment   74
    Styling from Camera View   74
    Following Your Instincts   74
Styling Tips and Tricks   76
    Adding Bulk   76
    Using Garnishes   79
    A Little Mess Is Okay   80
    Real Ice vs. Fake Ice   80
    Adding Movement   82
Prop Styling   84
    Relevance and Simplicity   85
    Dishes and Accessories   86
    Textiles and Textures   89
Chapter 3 Challenges   93

CHAPTER 4: FRAMING AND COMPOSITION 95

Improve Your Photos with Strong Compositional Elements

Poring Over the Picture	96
Poring Over the Picture	98
Finding Balance	100
The Rule of Thirds	100
Background and Foreground	101
Triangles and Groups of Threes	102
Perspective and Framing	104
Vertical and Horizontal	104
Three-Quarters	106
Eye Level	108
Overhead View	108
Focal Length, Lens Compression, and Depth of Field	110
What Is Lens Compression?	110
Why Focal Length Matters	110
Focus	112
Finding the Best Focus Point	113
Focusing Tips and Tricks	115
Shapes, Lines, and Colors	115
Shapes	115
Lines and Corners	115
Colors	117
Chapter 4 Challenges	119

CHAPTER 5: LET'S GET SOCIAL 121

Setting Yourself Up for Online Success

Poring Over the Picture	122
Poring Over the Picture	124
Your Website Is Your Online Home	126
Setting Up a Website and Blog	126
Setting Up Your Portfolio	128
Sharing and Networking	129
Grow a Social Media Presence	130
Build a Mailing List	131
Attend Conferences	133
Protecting Your Digital Content	134
Register Your Copyright	134
Use Watermarks on Images	136
Protect Your Blog	141
Words of Wisdom	144
Chapter 5 Challenge	145

CHAPTER 6: PROCESSING IMAGES WITH ADOBE LIGHTROOM   **147**

Making Your Photographs Look Their Best

Poring Over Adobe Lightroom   148
Getting Started   152
    Calibrating Your Monitor   152
    Photo-Editing Software   153
    Working in Adobe Lightroom   153
The Library Module   154
    Creating a Catalog   154
    Importing Your Files   154
    Organization Tips   162
    Selecting Keepers   165
The Develop Module   171
    Cropping and Cloning   171
    Basic Edits   173
    Working with Presets   183
Exporting Your Files   186
    Prepping for Export   186
    The Export Window   187
    Working with Export Presets   191
Chapter 6 Challenges   193

CHAPTER 7: BEHIND THE SCENES   **195**

Photographing Food from Start to Finish

Poring Over the Picture   196
Poring Over the Picture   198
Appetizers   201
    Props and Styling   204
    Lighting Setup   207
    Postprocessing   209
Green Mango Smoothie   215
    Props and Styling   215
    Lighting Setup   218
    Postprocessing   221
Grapefruit Salad   227
    Props and Styling   227
    Lighting Setup   232
    Postprocessing   234

Khao Soi   241
    Props and Styling   242
    Lighting Setup   246
    Postprocessing   248

CONCLUSION   **253**

INDEX   **254**

Introduction

Three years ago, I wrote the first edition of this book (*Food Photography: From Snapshots to Great Shots*). It was a book that I had in my head for quite some time, and Peachpit Press was willing to give me a chance with it. The response was so much more than I had anticipated, and while writing it (and throughout the years that followed), I became more and more infatuated with food photography.

Another thing that happened over the past few years is that my own personal style and attitude toward food photography has evolved and become much more refined. I light my food differently, use different props and plates, have taken a much more minimalistic approach toward my postprocessing, and use Adobe Lightroom instead of Adobe Photoshop. Because of these things, I decided that it was time to refresh my first book with a second edition, which has now become the book you are reading this very moment.

I hope you find this book useful as you make your way on your own journey through the world of food photography. Inside this book you will learn about some basic photography and lighting techniques, food styling, how to have an online presence through social media, as well as how to process your images using Adobe Lightroom.

In the end, we all develop our own style of photography, but one thing rings true when photographing food: It needs to look delicious. The purpose of this book is to guide photographers at all levels to make their food look as good as it tastes and to do so as naturally, organically, and simply as possible.

Here is a quick Q&A about the book to help you understand what you'll see in the following pages:

Q: What can I expect to learn from this book?

A: This book starts with the basics of photography (photographic fundamentals and equipment) and works through the steps of lighting, styling, composing, and editing the photographs. It shows how to present the food that you've cooked and prepared and turn it into a mouth-watering photograph.

Q: How does this book differ from the first edition?

A: In this edition, I wanted to make certain that those of you who already have my first edition will still get your money's worth. The first few chapters may seem a little similar (there's only so much to be written about the basics of photography and lighting for food); however, you will find nearly all of the photos have been replaced, and the last three chapters (almost half of the book) have been completely rewritten! I also updated certain chapters to better suit my current style in props and food styling.

Q: Who is this book written for?

A: Ultimately, this book is for anyone who wants to create beautiful food photographs. I wrote it with food bloggers and home cooks in mind, but all of the techniques can be used by photographers, cooks, or chefs of any type or skill level in any situation or environment.

Q: Should I read the book straight through or can I skip around from chapter to chapter?

A: There's really no set way to read the book. If you're new to photography, however, I recommend that you read the first few chapters to get an understanding of the basics and build a solid foundation of photography before diving in to the lighting and food-specific information. If you're a fairly seasoned photographer who understands your camera and most of the basic techniques, then you can jump straight to the more food-specific chapters.

Q: What are the challenges all about?

A: At the end of most chapters, I list a few exercises that will help you practice and solidify some of the techniques and settings you learned about. Feel free to try them out if you like, and if you do, be sure to get online and share your photographs! I would *love* to see them.

1
Food Photography Fundamentals

The Tools and Setup for Digital Food Photography

When it comes to photographing food, the basics of digital photography are really no different from those for other photographic genres. It's important to have a solid understanding of such basics as exposure and white balance, as well as the camera gear you will use before venturing into food photography. In this chapter, I will discuss some of the essentials you need to create mouth-watering images.

An old, painted-wood tabletop helps add texture to the scene.

Canon 5D Mark III ·
ISO 100 · 1/8 sec. ·
ƒ/5.6 · Canon 100mm
ƒ/2.8L Macro lens

I love to photograph (and eat) small, bite-sized appetizers. For this setup, I prepared several different plates of food to add variety and interest to all parts of the photograph. I also chose a bright blue plate for the main subject to bring out the beautiful warm colors in the salmon.

Additional food elements were added to the plate to balance the composition of the appetizers.

Poring Over the Picture

I love photographing berries, and I try to add them to my photographs whenever I get the chance. This particular dish, a "dessert bruschetta" of sorts, appealed to me because of the beautiful textures, layers, and colors that were created when all of the ingredients were put together.

I added some fresh blueberries to the plate to add balance and color.

Canon 5D Mark III •
ISO 100 • 1/4 sec. •
ƒ/6.7 • Canon 100mm
ƒ/2.8L Macro lens

A fresh sprig of mint adds brightness and color to the photograph.

I was careful to frame the elements in the background so that they did not "intersect" with the main subject.

Digital Cameras

There are a lot of cameras out there. A *lot*. New ones pop up on the market every year, and the technology keeps improving and changing—sometimes so quickly that it's difficult to keep up. There are three types of cameras that you're likely familiar with (and might already own): P&S (point-and-shoot), DSLR (digital single-lens reflex), and mirrorless.

The Limitations of the P&S

The point-and-shoot camera is pretty much summed up by its name: point and shoot. There are honestly too many on the market these days to count, and they're all different in their own ways. Some are simple with few options or settings to choose from, and others are so complicated and advanced that they are virtually on par with an interchangeable-lens camera.

You may be wondering whether you can get a good photograph, more specifically a good *food* photograph, from a P&S. My answer is…maybe. On occasion you can get a similar photograph from a point-and-shoot when compared to a camera with interchangeable lenses. Because of the nature of a P&S, however, you will have much less control over the camera, specifically with depth of field and focal length (**Figures 1.1** and **1.2**).

The main reason that P&S cameras are so limited is that the lens is permanently attached to the camera body. They also have a small sensor, which can equate to a lower-quality image when compared to a DSLR or mirrorless camera. Another downside to P&S cameras is that they typically give you little control with your exposure, and possibly even with your focus point. You're usually limited to choosing among several different "auto" modes that select your shutter speed and aperture. Some cameras do offer a few of the manual and semi-manual modes, but many don't offer those options.

Figure 1.1
This image was photographed with a point-and-shoot camera. The quality is not bad, even at a high ISO. However, the depth of field in the background is not as shallow as I would prefer it to be, even when zoomed in all the way and at a large aperture of $f/2.8$.

Sony DSC-RX100 III · ISO 1600 · 1/20 sec. · $f/2.8$ ·
Focal length (full-frame equivalent): 70mm

Figure 1.2
Compare this image with its point-and-shoot counterpart. Notice that even at a higher aperture value ($f/5.6$) the background is significantly more blurred.

Canon 5D Mark III · ISO 100 · 1/4 sec. · $f/5.6$ ·
Canon 100mm $f/2.8$L Macro lens

Mobile Phones for Food Photography

One option that I do use quite often with food, which could in its own right be considered a P&S, is a mobile phone. Specifically, I use an iPhone. Having the ability to quickly create a photo and then share it online can be a huge benefit for marketing, social media, or maybe just a simple blog post. Mobile phones oftentimes have limitations, however, such as their inability to create a good photograph in low-light conditions (without using the harsh, ugly flash, that is). If you do choose to use your phone for food photography, I encourage you to properly light and present your food in a way that allows you to avoid these types of obstacles (**Figure 1.3**).

Figure 1.3
When I photograph food with my iPhone, I tend to compose it from overhead. I find that it creates a more pleasing composition and helps overcome some of the obstacles faced with point-and-shoot cameras.

iPhone 5 · ISO 64 · 1/20 sec. · ƒ/2.4 ·
Focal length (full-frame equivalent): 44mm

iPhone 6 Plus · ISO 100 · 1/4 sec. · ƒ/2.2 ·
Focal length (full-frame equivalent): 44mm

iPhone 6 Plus · ISO 40 · 1/30 sec. · ƒ/2.2 ·
Focal length (full-frame equivalent): 39mm

iPhone 6 Plus · ISO 32 · 1/15 sec. · ƒ/2.2 ·
Focal length (full-frame equivalent): 39mm

DSLR and Mirrorless

The two professional-grade cameras currently on the market are the DSLR and mirrorless styles (**Figure 1.4**). The main difference between these two cameras is size. DSLR cameras are built so that they have a mirror behind the lens, which then reflects the light (and what is visible from the lens) up through a chamber and into the viewfinder. The mirrorless camera removes this entire portion from the camera (which is why it's called "mirrorless"), and it shows a digital representation of what you are photographing in the viewfinder instead of an "optical" representation. This, in turn, allows the camera to be much lighter and compact in size with comparable levels of quality (**Figures 1.5A** and **B**).

Figure 1.4
This is a Canon 5D Mark III (with Canon 40mm pancake lens) side-by-side with a Fuji X-T1 (with Zeiss 32mm f/1.8 lens).

A   B

Figure 1.5
The DSLR photograph (A) shows little difference in quality compared to the mirrorless camera's version of the same subject (B).

(A) Canon 5D Mark III · ISO 100 · 1/4 sec. · f/8 · Canon 100mm f/2.8L Macro lens
(B) Fuji X-T1 · ISO 200 · 1/8 sec. · f/5.6 · Fuji 18–135mm f/3.5–5.6 lens

These two types of cameras have more similarities than differences, with the biggest being that many of them allow you to change the lens (with a few fixed-lens exceptions for some mirrorless cameras). This makes them the preferred tools for most serious photographers. Both DSLR and mirrorless cameras offer the photographer an enormous amount of control with exposure, focus point, and lens choice. What's also great about them is that when you look through the viewfinder, you are seeing the exact photograph you will be taking. This may not be a big deal these days, however, because most digital cameras offer live-view options that allow you to see through the lens by looking at an LCD monitor on the back of the camera.

Another advantage to DSLR and mirrorless cameras is their larger sensor size. Most interchangeable-lens cameras come with either a full-frame sensor or a crop sensor—keep reading to learn the differences between the two different types of sensors available on today's DSLR and mirrorless cameras.

Full-Frame versus Crop Sensor

Digital cameras typically have one of two types of sensors: full-frame or crop. All *full-frame* sensors have an area of 36 x 24mm, which is the same size as a 35mm negative. A *crop* sensor is approximately 23 x 15mm, but the exact dimensions will differ based on camera brand and model (**Figure 1.6**).

Figure 1.6
This image was photographed with a full-frame camera. The inside grid represents the area that would be in the frame if the fruit was photographed with a crop-frame camera.

Canon 5D Mark III ·
ISO 100 · 2 sec. ·
ƒ/5.6 · Canon 100mm
ƒ/2.8L Macro lens

It's important to understand the distinctions between these two types of sensors because there are significant differences in how each sensor size affects focal length and sometimes even the image quality. When you use a 200mm lens on a full-frame sensor, what you see through the viewfinder is actually at 200mm. When you use the same lens on a crop-sensor camera, however, you see the equivalent of a 320mm lens. So with a crop-sensor camera, you basically see a "cropped-in" or "magnified" version of what you would see with a full-frame camera (**Figures 1.7** and **1.8**).

Figure 1.7
This image represents a scene photographed with a full-frame camera.

Figure 1.8
This is the same setup as in Figure 1.7 but photographed with a crop-frame camera. Notice how the scene appears to be "zoomed in." To fit the entirety of the scene in the frame, you would need to move the camera further from the table.

Canon 5D Mark III · ISO 100 · 1/2 sec. · ƒ/5.6 · Canon 100mm ƒ/2.8L Macro lens

Canon 70D · ISO 100 · 0.8 sec. · ƒ/5.6 · Canon 100mm ƒ/2.8L Macro lens

As always, both cameras offer advantages and disadvantages. A full-frame camera offers a much larger angle of view, so you can capture more information in your photograph. This is particularly useful with wide-angle lenses because you can get *really* wide when using these lenses. You're also likely to have more megapixels with full-frame cameras, and those megapixels are spread out over a larger area, which can result in lower noise and higher image quality when you look closely at the pixels.

With crop-sensor cameras, as I mentioned earlier, your area of view is "cropped in," so each lens you use has a higher *effective focal length*, meaning the focal length you actually see through the lens. For example, using a 100mm lens on a crop-sensor camera with a crop factor of 1.6 gives you an effective focal length of 160mm.

I find both types of sensors useful and different. For some photographers, the "advantages" of the full-frame may seem like a disadvantage if they prefer tighter, more zoomed-in crops of their images. Most of the "pro" camera bodies are full-frame, while the entry-level and "semi-pro" bodies tend to be crop-sensor, but don't let those labels sway you when deciding what to use for your food photography. I have used both full-frame and crop-sensor cameras for my food photography with comparable results in every single instance.

Which Camera Should I Buy?

This is one of the questions most asked by new photographers. If you're new to this industry, you're probably scratching your head with confusion— there are just so many cameras to choose from! My advice would be to start small. If you have a few requirements for a camera, then stick with those, but don't spend money on the most expensive camera on the market. Often those models are expensive for a few specific features— such as high speed (the number of frames it can photograph in one second) or the number of megapixels—that you may not even need.

On the other hand, if you definitely want a DSLR or mirrorless camera, don't buy a point-and-shoot camera just because it's less expensive. Once you start really getting into photography, you'll slowly understand your photographic style and be able to tailor-fit a camera that suits your specific needs.

It's also important to understand that while you'll probably go through several camera bodies in your lifetime as a photographer, you're likely to keep the same lenses. Good, quality lenses (also referred to as *glasses*) are usually considered more important to photographers than the camera body they're using. So read on for more information on the different types of lenses and focal lengths you can use.

Lenses and Focal Lengths

The lens is the "eye" of the camera. It determines the widest aperture you can use, and the quality of the glass in the lens determines the sharpness and overall clarity of your final image.

Lens choice is a personal decision, and lenses can often help photographers develop their own unique style. I know that I have my favorites when it comes to food photography, but I also carry other lenses in my camera bag just in case.

Wide-Angle

Wide-angle lenses have an extremely wide angle of view. They're popular in landscape photography and on those occasions when you need to show a lot of information in a scene. They cover a field of view from about 110 degrees to about 60 degrees; focal lengths of 35mm and smaller are considered to be wide lenses (**Figures 1.9** and **1.10**).

When it comes to food photography, I honestly don't use wide-angle lenses often and typically will go wide only if I'm shooting from overhead. You have to be extremely careful if you use one because wide-angle lenses can add distortion to an image, an effect that is usually not pleasing with food. Another consideration is that wide-angle lenses have a greater depth of field when compared to longer focal lengths. So, if you're going for a soft, background that has an out-of-focus look, then using these lenses is probably not your best choice.

Figure 1.9
Wide-angle lenses are not always the best choice for food photography, especially when photographing a small setup like these small citrus slices.

Canon 5D Mark III · ISO 100 · 1/8 sec. · ƒ/6.7 · Canon 24–70mm ƒ/2.8L lens · Focal length: 24mm

Figure 1.10
I find that wide lenses work best when photographing a setup from overhead.

Canon 5D Mark III · ISO 100 · 1/4 sec. · ƒ/6.7 · Canon 24–70mm ƒ/2.8L lens · Focal length: 35mm

Midrange

The focal length of a midrange lens can be anywhere between 35mm and 80mm, with 50mm being the most common. The perspective you see with these lenses is natural and will introduce little (if any) distortion to your photographs (**Figures 1.11** and **1.12**).

With normal focal lengths, you can usually create shallow depth of field to blur the background, depending on the aperture setting and the distance between the subject and its background. This is known as *lens compression* (see Chapter 4 for more information). I think that every photographer should have at least one inexpensive 40mm or 50mm prime lens in their camera bag.

Figure 1.11
This dish was photographed with a 50mm lens.

Canon 5D Mark III · ISO 100 · 1/2 sec. · ƒ/4 ·
Canon 50mm ƒ/2.5 Macro lens

Figure 1.12
Midrange focal lengths are great options for overhead shots because they create minimal distortion in the scene.

Canon 5D Mark III · ISO 100 · 1/4 sec. · ƒ/6.7 ·
Canon 24–70mm ƒ/2.8L lens · Focal length: 70mm

Telephoto

Telephoto lenses are great when you want to photograph something that is far away but make it appear very close. The focal lengths of these lenses usually start at 100mm and go all the way up to the "super telephoto" range of 300mm and beyond. Telephoto lenses are popular in portrait, wedding, and nature photography.

It's likely that you won't have much of a need for a *super* telephoto lens with food photography, but you might find that a lens at the lower telephoto range can add a nice amount of blur to your photographs because of the shallow depth of field they can create. I have many images that I photographed at the 200mm range because I love the compression—the ability to alter the perspective of a photo and make the background appear closer to the subject—and blur that the lens adds to the backgrounds (**Figure 1.13**).

To further increase the focal length of a lens, you can also use a *telephoto extender*. This adds extra magnification to your lens so that it will "reach" a little bit further. Be aware that you might lose a little bit of sharpness in your photograph, and it also will change the maximum aperture setting on your lens. For example, if you have a lens that opens up all the way to $f/4$ at the largest setting, adding a 1.4x extender to the lens will change it so the widest aperture will be $f/5.6$.

Prime and Zoom Lenses

A *prime* lens is a lens at a fixed focal length, like 50mm or 85mm. Some photographers prefer to use only prime lenses because they can create sharper focus points and are much faster to focus. A *zoom* lens, on the other hand, is a lens that has a range of focal lengths, like 18–55mm or 70–200mm. Because zoom lenses have more moving parts than prime lenses, they can create a slightly softer focus and may be slower. But on the flip side, their different focal lengths offer a lot of flexibility.

Note

See Chapter 4 for more information on how to compress an image using a longer focal length.

Macro Lenses

The macro lens is another good choice for dedicated food photographers. Using a macro lens allows greater flexibility, especially when photographing small items. The intention with using a macro when photographing food is not to get extremely close to the subject but rather to properly fill the frame. Some lenses, especially on a full-frame camera, will not allow the camera to focus at close distances, which is why the macro lens is my lens of choice for food photography.

One of my personal favorite lenses to use with food photography is a 100mm macro lens, which I use in conjunction with a Canon 5D Mark III camera. This focal length allows me to compress and blur the background to my liking, and it is also helpful when I want to photograph smaller items (**Figures 1.14** and **1.15**). It is also a prime lens, so it is tack-sharp when focused properly.

Figure 1.13
A telephoto lens is a good option if you want to add a lot of blur to your background.

Canon 5D Mark III •
ISO 100 • 0.3 sec. •
ƒ/5.6 • Canon
70–200mm
ƒ/4L IS lens •
Focal length: 200mm

Figure 1.14
Because this food
was small, I needed
a macro lens to get
in close enough to
fill the frame.

Canon 5D Mark III •
ISO 100 • 1/4 sec. •
ƒ/5.6 • Canon 100mm
ƒ/2.8L Macro lens

Figure 1.15
A macro lens is also
a good option when
doing ingredient shots
because they are usually
much smaller than the
prepared dish.

Canon 5D Mark III •
ISO 100 • 6 sec. •
ƒ/5.6 • Canon 100mm
ƒ/2.8L Macro lens

The Lensbaby

Another lens I like to use is the Lensbaby Composer Pro, a unique lens with a range of optics that allows you to get creative with your photographs. For instance, this lens can mimic the effects of a tilt-shift lens and can introduce a unique blur to images. The Composer Pro (http://lensbaby.com) comes with several different optics, which enable you to alter the type of photographic effect. For food photography, my preference is to use the Edge 80, which mimics a tilt-shift look (**Figure 1.16**). This can be a fun lens to experiment with in food photography, and what's great about it is that it's inexpensive when compared to most specialty lenses.

Figure 1.16
This image was photographed with a Lensbaby to give it a tilt-shift look. Notice how the in-focus area starts at the bottom and angles up to the top on the right side of the frame, which is characteristic of tilt-shift lenses.

Canon 5D Mark III · ISO 100 · 0.3 sec. · ƒ/5.6 · Lensbaby Composer Pro, Edge 80 Optic, Macro Converter

Tripods and Accessories

With photography and camera gear, there will always be those extra things that you'll find useful when creating your photographs. Some of them are essential, and others are just for fun. Here are a few that I use regularly when photographing food.

Tripods and Camera Stands

A tripod is an invaluable piece of equipment for almost any type of photography. Some photographers use them more frequently than others, and some food photographers use them constantly for their work. Although I have been known to hold the camera in my hand for some of my food photographs, I almost *always* use my tripod when I'm working with diffused window light because the shutter speed will usually be too slow for hand-held photography. A tripod is also useful when you have a specific composition in mind and need to stage your scene carefully.

There are many, many different types of tripods for a variety of purposes. Some tripods are heavy, some are light, and both have advantages and disadvantages. Just as you would with a camera, you'll want to determine what your specific needs are before deciding what to get. The heavier the tripod, the more difficult it is to transport, but it will also be a lot sturdier and will keep your photographs free of camera shake. Lighter tripods, such as well-built carbon fiber tripods, can be handy when you want to carry them around, but they will also be more expensive. Tripods that are very light (think "made of plastic") are more likely to introduce camera shake into images, however, and some are even too light to hold many of the large DSLR cameras and lenses.

My inventory of tripods consists of an extremely heavy tripod that pretty much stays put and doesn't get lugged around too often, as well as a much lighter carbon-fiber tripod that I travel with a lot. I use both of them, and I actually prefer the larger, heavier one for much of my food photography because of its sturdiness—but I sure wouldn't want to pack it for a day hike.

Tripod Heads

If you're using a tripod, then you're also going to need a tripod head. The tripod head is an accessory that mounts to the top of the tripod and is the place where you will actually attach your camera. As with everything else, a lot of options are available, and you usually get what you pay for. You can find them in many varieties—ball heads, video heads, pan heads, and so on. I recommend stopping by your local camera store to check them out and see how they all work.

I've found that although quality is an important consideration (you don't want your camera sliding around on its own), ergonomics is almost equally important. You want to find a tripod head that is easy for you to maneuver and position. My current favorite is a three-way pan/tilt head that allows me to adjust each axis separately. This gives me the exact control I need, especially when creating an intricate food setup. I also use a bracket from Custom Brackets (www.custombrackets.com) that allows me to quickly go from a horizontal to vertical orientation in no time at all (**Figure 1.17**).

Cable Releases

A cable release is a cord that attaches to your camera and allows you to press the shutter without actually touching the camera, a useful tool when your camera is attached to a tripod (**Figure 1.18**). When you're using a slow shutter speed, just pressing the shutter button on the camera can shake it enough to blur your photograph; a cable release pretty much guarantees that this won't happen. If you don't have one, you can always use your camera's self-timer mode, but even though you have to wait just a few seconds for each photograph, you'll probably become impatient and want to get a cable release. Plus, that gorgeous food won't look beautiful forever—every second counts!

Figure 1.17
My current tripod setup consists of an old, sturdy tripod (the Manfrotto 325, www.manfrotto .com), a Benro 3-Way Panhead (www .benrousa.com), and the Digital Pro SV from Custom Brackets, which allows me to swivel the camera from horizontal to vertical without removing it from the tripod.

Figure 1.18
I always use a cable release when photographing food on a tripod.

Working with Digital Files

When using a digital camera, you will need to work with the digital files to get a finished product. Creating the photograph can sometimes be the easiest part, but if you're new to photography, you may be a bit lost when the time comes to processing your photos. In this section, I will discuss some of the basics to consider when creating an image, and then in Chapter 6 I will show you step-by-step how to process your images using Adobe Light-room (www.adobe.com).

RAW vs. JPEG

When photographing with a digital camera, you usually have the choice of file formats: RAW or JPEG. Some older cameras may create JPEG images only, but pretty much all cameras that use interchangeable lenses and allow you to see exactly what you are photographing enable you to photograph in the RAW format as well.

The main difference between RAW and JPEG is the range of ability you have to process your photo after you capture the image. A RAW file gives you greater flexibility and allows you to nondestructively edit the photo (meaning you won't permanently change the file and can restart your processing at any time). JPEG files, on the other hand, have the settings "baked in." Sure, you can make changes, such as adding a little bit of brightness or contrast here and there, but you can do only so much before it starts to negatively impact the pixels in the photo.

One of the biggest advantages to shooting RAW over JPEG is the ability to adjust the white balance while processing the image in Lightroom or Adobe Photoshop. A properly color-balanced image is essential in food photography, and if the colors are off when shooting in RAW, then you can just make a few adjustments on the computer to balance it out.

Here's my advice: I highly recommend that you shoot in the RAW format. In fact, when I photograph food, I use RAW 100 percent of the time. If you are still uncomfortable with postprocessing and know that the JPEG may give you a faster (or easier) image to work with, then set your camera to shoot in RAW+JPEG, which will give you an identical copy of the same image in both formats.

Advantages of RAW:

- Wide dynamic range

- Ability to change white balance in editing

- Ease in making nondestructive edits

Disadvantages of RAW:

- Large file size

- Additional software and editing experience required

Who benefits from using RAW?

- Photographers who have large enough memory cards, want the best-quality image they can create, and can take the time to edit each of their images on their computers

Advantages of JPEG:

- Smaller file size

- Little editing required

Disadvantages of JPEG:

- Editing may cause loss in details and image quality

- Exposure and white balance must be extremely accurate in-camera

Who benefits from using JPEG?

- Photographers who need smaller files, can get their exposure and white balance close to perfect in-camera, and want to do little (if any) editing on their computers

White Balance

White balance is an important fundamental to understand, especially with food photography, because it deals with color balance in the image, and a food's colors can greatly affect its visual appeal. It's called white balance because the overall intent is to make sure that the whites are actually white and that the balance of color in the photograph is true to its original color, depending on the type of light in which it was photographed.

To get a bit deeper into this (without going too geeky), I'll start by defining white balance and why we have it. Let's say you are using the Auto white balance setting. Basically, different light sources give off different temperatures of light, measured in Kelvin. Your camera measures the color of the light you are photographing; then it determines which Kelvin temperature to use in-camera so that the color of your image is as true to the scene's natural state as possible. But you can also choose the setting in advance, if you know the type of light you will be shooting in. The settings on digital cameras usually have names such as Cloudy, Daylight, Fluorescent, or Tungsten (**Figure 1.19**). Most of the time these are just averages of what the color balances typically look like in each of these situations. There's also a setting on most cameras that lets you dial in the specific Kelvin temperature of the light, if you know it.

Auto

Daylight

Cloudy

Shade

Tungsten

Fluorescent

Flash

Figure 1.19
This set of images, lit with diffused window light, represents the different white balance settings. You can see that the Daylight, Shade, Cloudy, and Flash settings all produce decent results, mostly because they are based on daylight-balanced light, and only slight adjustments would be needed when editing. The Tungsten and Fluorescent results, however, are less than desirable.

Canon 5D Mark II · ISO 100 · 1/15 sec. · ƒ/5.6 · Canon 100mm ƒ/2.8L Macro lens

When photographing food, the majority of the time you will probably be working in daylight, whether it's shaded sunlight or off-camera flash/strobe; if so, you could pick from the Daylight, Shade, or Cloudy white balance settings and probably get pretty close to a desirable color balance. If you were to ask me what I do, I'd tell you that I usually just keep my white balance setting on Auto (**Figure 1.20**). Newer cameras tend to do a good job getting an accurate white balance, often requiring only minor adjustments in the editing process.

Figure 1.20
I almost always photograph my food using the Auto, or AWB (auto white balance), setting.

As much as I loathe saying "you can fix it on the computer," this is one of those settings that I really don't sweat about until I'm sitting in front of my computer, mostly because Auto white balance usually does a pretty good job to begin with. It's also something that I almost always adjust while editing, even if the white balance was customized as I created the image in my camera. If you are using JPEG, however, you'll really want to make sure that this setting is as accurate as possible, because you don't have as much wiggle room to work with in postprocessing.

If you do want to achieve an accurate (or close to accurate) custom white balance setting, there are tools you can buy or create to get you pretty close. A simple gray card, white piece of paper, disposable white plastic coffee lid, or perfectly color-balanced white-balancing device can usually get your images close to where you want them. Consult your camera's user manual for more information on setting up a custom white balance.

The Exposure Triangle: Aperture, Shutter Speed, and ISO

To create a photograph you need light. To get that light with the proper exposure, you need to balance three camera settings: aperture, shutter speed, and ISO. Your goal in using these elements is to find a good balance of light, depth of field, and focus, and while there are some principles to understand and follow, there's no set of rules or presets that you can use to always get the correct exposure. The key is to know how the settings work together so you can make your own creative decisions.

Aperture

The aperture is the element in a lens that allows the light to pass through it and into the camera, ultimately reaching the sensor. Aperture controls two things: the amount of light coming into the lens and the depth of field. To control the light you change the physical size of the aperture. It looks like a circle but is actually made up of blades that fan in and out to decrease and increase the aperture's size. When opened wide, the aperture lets a lot of light in, and when tightened to be small, it lets little light pass. The actual size limits of the aperture depend on the capabilities of each particular lens.

To set the aperture, you select an f-stop number—a smaller number equals a wide opening, which means more light coming through the lens; a larger number equals a smaller opening and less light coming through the lens. The easiest way to remember this is to think of the numbers as fractions, where f/2 is going to be bigger than f/16, for example. A lens with an extremely wide opening is considered a "fast" lens and is typically more expensive, too. The benefits of using fast lenses are that not only do you have more light to work with, but you have enormous control over

Sensor

The camera sensor is the light-sensitive area within the camera that converts the optical signal of your image into digital data. If you're familiar with film photography, think of it as the piece of film that is exposed to create the negative.

depth of field. A fast lens photographing at its widest aperture creates a shallow depth of field but also allows you to tighten the aperture if a wide aperture isn't required (for example, to move from f/2.8 to f/8 or smaller). Another great thing about fast lenses is that they give you flexibility in low-light situations, especially when handholding your camera. You do need to be careful when focusing a lens that is set to a wide aperture, however, because it's likely that much of the image will be out of focus.

Shutter Speed

Before I get into defining shutter speed, first let's discuss what the shutter does and how it works inside the camera. Remember that the aperture is the opening inside the lens that controls the amount of light entering the camera. Now, think of the shutter as a door or curtain inside the camera, directly in front of a sensor, that opens and closes to allow the light from the aperture to actually expose the sensor and create the photograph.

The shutter speed setting literally determines how long the shutter stays open. With a fast shutter speed, the shutter will be open for only a brief period of time, thereby allowing little light to hit the sensor. When opened for a longer period of time, it allows more light to reach the sensor. A fast shutter speed will "freeze" action and allow you to handhold the camera, whereas a long shutter speed will capture movement in the frame (if there is any) and will almost always require the camera to be on a tripod (**Figure 1.21**).

Figure 1.21
The movement of this dripping honey was blurred due to a slow shutter speed.

Canon 5D Mark III •
ISO 100 • 1/4 sec. •
ƒ/5.6 • Canon 100mm
ƒ/2.8L Macro lens

Depth of Field

Depth of field describes how much of your image is actually in focus. If an image has great depth of field, the majority of the photograph is in focus (**Figure 1.22**). In an image with little (or shallow) depth of field, there is usually a selective point of focus with the foreground and/or background out of focus (or blurry); this is usually achieved with a combination of a longer focal length and a wide aperture (**Figure 1.23**). Controlling the depth of field in an image is a useful creative tool and one that I consider extremely important in my own photography.

Figure 1.22
Using a small aperture (in this example, _f_/32) gives your image a greater depth of field.

Canon 5D Mark III · ISO 100 · 3 sec. · _f_/32 · Canon 100mm _f_/2.8L Macro lens

Figure 1.23
A larger aperture, such as _f_/4, adds more blur to your background for a shallow depth of field.

Canon 5D Mark III · ISO 100 · 1/15 sec. · _f_/4.5 · Canon 100mm _f_/2.8L Macro lens

Shutter speed is measured in seconds and fractions of seconds. A fraction of a second might seem pretty fast, and it is, but you'd be surprised at how much movement you can introduce into images with settings like 1/15 and 1/30 of a second. With a stationary object, the shutter speed is really irrelevant as far as the final product is concerned, especially if you are using a tripod. But there may be times when you want to add movement to your image (or prevent movement), so it's important to understand how shutter speed works.

Note

See Chapter 2 for more information on using lights in food photography.

When photographing food, it's likely that you'll be more concerned, creatively speaking, with the aperture setting to control depth of field and that you'll determine the shutter speed by how much light is still required to properly expose the image. With a typical DSLR and a 50mm lens, you can safely handhold your camera at a shutter speed of 1/60 of a second, and maybe even 1/30 of a second, depending on how steady your hands are. Anything longer than that will require a tripod because handholding a long exposure can introduce camera shake and blurred movement that you might not want to see in your image. Also, if you are using a lens with a longer focal length, you'll have to increase this "base level" of handheld shutter speed because the longer the lens, the more movement you can introduce in your image. A good rule of thumb is to use the same shutter speed as your focal length: If you are using a 100mm lens, then you should try to keep your shutter speed at or above 1/125 of a second (1/100 of a second isn't an actual shutter speed). This, of course, will depend on you and the type of light you are using. If you are using studio lights or off-camera strobes, for example, then the shutter speed is dependent on the shutter sync speed of your camera.

ISO

The final element of exposure is ISO. ISO is an acronym for the International Organization for Standardization and is used as a term to describe the sensitivity of the camera's sensor to light. ISO numbers usually start at 100 and can go up to 12,800 (or even higher, depending on your camera). The lower the number is, the less sensitive to light; the higher the number, the more sensitive to light. So, if you have your ISO set to 100, you would need more light to create a proper exposure than you would with a setting of ISO 800, for example.

Now, if you're creating an image and have set your aperture and shutter speed but then realize you need more light, you may be tempted to just crank the ISO way up so that the sensor is more sensitive, allowing you to create your photograph with no other changes. Unfortunately, it's not that simple. You see, there's a disadvantage to using an extremely high ISO: noise. With a low number, you'll see little noise; however, the higher that number gets, the more noise you will see in your images (**Figure 1.24**).

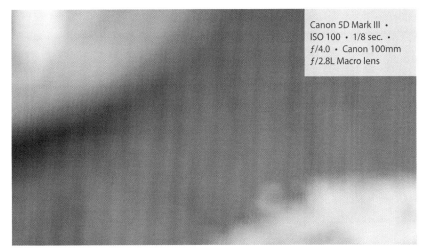

Canon 5D Mark III · ISO 100 · 1/8 sec. · f/4.0 · Canon 100mm f/2.8L Macro lens

Figure 1.24
In these three examples, you can see how using a high ISO will impact the noise in a photograph. I cropped each of these images to 100% to show the noise much more clearly.

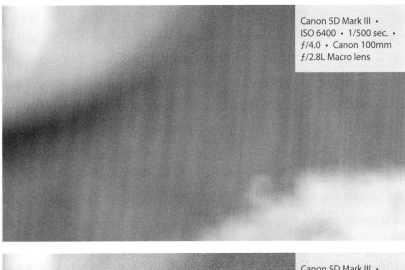

Canon 5D Mark III · ISO 6400 · 1/500 sec. · f/4.0 · Canon 100mm f/2.8L Macro lens

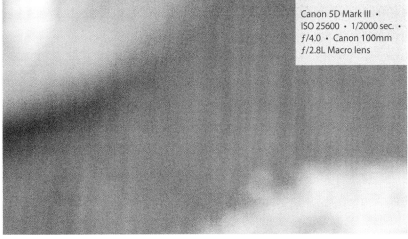

Canon 5D Mark III · ISO 25600 · 1/2000 sec. · f/4.0 · Canon 100mm f/2.8L Macro lens

The amount of noise you actually see in your images will also be determined by the final output of your photograph. If you plan to use your photos only as low-resolution digital images on a website, then you can probably get away with increasing the ISO number. The larger you view the image, the more clearly you will see its noise, and web images are typically small. Ultimately, the acceptable amount of noise in your images is up to you. If you have the resources, light, and ability to create your images at a low ISO, that's usually a good choice. But if you're in an environment where you have no option but to increase the ISO and the content of the photograph is more important than the quality, then, by all means, do what you have to do to make the photograph. For my images, especially food photographs, I do my best to photograph everything at ISO 100, the lowest native ISO level my camera allows, to ensure a crisp, clean, noise-free image.

Calculating Overall Exposure

As I mentioned at the beginning of this section, each of the components of the exposure triangle—aperture, shutter speed, and ISO—need to be balanced to create a proper exposure. Now that you know what they are and how they determine exposure, you might still be wondering where to start. How are you supposed to know where to set each of the settings to create a properly exposed photograph? The thing is, there's no single way to create a photograph, and there's definitely not a right way. Creating a proper exposure is about balancing each of the elements to get the look and feel *you* want out of your photographs.

To start, you'll likely be using the meter inside your camera (**Figure 1.25**). The overall goal of this meter is to balance all of these elements so that what it sees, tonally speaking, is gray. Here's an easy way to test this out. Take your camera (make sure the flash is turned off) and point it at a white wall. Don't worry about the settings for now; just set it to Auto and take a photo. Now, look at the photo. Assuming there is nothing off with your settings, the image of your once-white wall that you are previewing on your camera is now likely a muddy gray. That's the camera's meter at work. It saw that white wall and tried to bring it back to a neutral gray. If you were to repeat the same experiment with a black surface, you would get similar results.

Figure 1.25
Using the meter inside your camera is a simple and accurate way to get a proper exposure when photographing in natural light.

As I mentioned earlier, there are many ways to create a proper exposure. Any single setting is interchangeable with different settings to create the same exposure, with what is called *reciprocal exposures*—that is, the images will look different, but the amount of light reaching the sensor is the same. This means that if your camera is set one way and you change one of the settings but want to maintain the same amount of light reaching the sensor, you would simply adjust the other two settings—whether aperture, shutter speed, or ISO—to balance it out. It's your job to adjust the settings to get the final creative look you want to achieve.

Reciprocal Exposures: ISO 100								
F-STOP	2.0	2.8	4	5.6	8	11	16	22
SHUTTER SPEED	1/8000	1/4000	1/2000	1/1000	1/500	1/250	1/125	1/60

Mastering the relationship of these elements of exposure in your photographs is the first step to understanding photography. If you can grasp the basics, the rest is easy—it's all just a matter of experimenting, playing around with your camera, and discovering your style and preferences.

What Camera Mode Should I Use?

You can use many different modes to control the exposure in your images. For food photography, I recommend using either Manual mode or Aperture Priority. Manual mode allows you full control over all of the settings, such as ISO, aperture, and shutter speed, and requires that you change those settings when the light in your scene changes as well. This is a good option to use, especially if you are photographing with strobes or off-camera flash.

Aperture Priority is another powerful setting, and it's the mode I use most frequently (especially when photographing in natural light). With the Aperture Priority mode, you determine the aperture setting and ISO, and the camera calculates the shutter speed. If shutter speed is not an important creative choice with your photograph, particularly if your subject is a non-moving plate of food, then I highly recommend considering the Aperture Priority setting. And, if you find that you need to under- or overexpose the scene to get it balanced, you can make adjustments with the Exposure Compensation setting in your camera (**Figure 1.26**).

Figure 1.26
When using Aperture Priority mode, you can increase or decrease your exposure by adjusting the Exposure Compensation dial.

Photographing Food in Live View

When my camera is on a tripod, I am almost guaranteed to be viewing my scene in Live View mode. Almost all cameras on the market give you this ability, and if you have it, then I highly suggest you make use of it. It is a great way to compose your scene without having to peek into the tiny viewfinder each time you make a change. It can also give you immediate feedback on your lighting setup, white balance, and use of reflectors, especially when photographing in natural light (**Figure 1.27**). Using Live View will tend to drain the battery a little faster, however, so be sure to have a few spare batteries charged and ready to go.

Figure 1.27
I prefer to use the Live View mode on my camera when photographing food on a tripod.

Chapter 1 Challenges

Understanding how to balance each of the basic elements—aperture, shutter speed, ISO, and white balance—to create a beautiful photograph can take a bit of time and patience, but it's an extremely important step in learning photography. In fact, it's probably one of the most important steps. Here are some exercises to get your brain moving in the right direction!

Experiment with Depth of Field

It's likely that you will want to blur the background of your food photographs if you are shooting them at eye-level, but sometimes too much blur is not a good thing. The best way to find that middle ground is to experiment! Set up a food shoot with your camera on a tripod and create several images of the same scene, all at different apertures. Then, compare each of them on the computer to see their pros and cons.

Zoom In, Then Go Wide

Set up a plate of food and try photographing it two different ways. First, use a normal or zoom lens to compose it so that the scene looks pleasing. Then, switch to a wide lens and try to frame the shot the same way. Pay attention to how the background changes as you go from a longer to a shorter focal length.

Blur Motion with a Slow Shutter Speed

Come up with a unique food setup where you can add an element of movement, such as pouring syrup or sprinkling powdered sugar. Then, place your camera on a tripod and make sure that the shutter speed is slow, such as 1/4 or 1/2 second. Then, take several photos while adding the movement to your scene and compare the photos. If you have enough light, try photographing it with a higher shutter speed so that you can see the difference.

Share your results with the book's Flickr group! Join the group here: flickr.com/groups/ foodphotographyfromsnapshotstogreatshots

Canon 5D Mark III •
ISO 100 • 1/4 sec. •
ƒ/4 • Canon 100mm
ƒ/2.8L Macro lens

2
Lighting

Techniques and Equipment for Lighting Food

Light is, hands down, the most important aspect of a photograph. The word *photography* means "to draw with light," so it won't come as much of a surprise when I tell you that this is probably the most important chapter in this book. But just because it's important doesn't mean it has to be overly complicated. I will often use a basic, simple lighting setup for my food photographs and make slight changes depending on the texture, height, and angles of the food. Your goal is to make the food stand out and look its best, so turn the page and keep reading to find out more about lighting food for photography.

Poring Over the Picture

I timed this photo perfectly to capture the syrup pouring right on top of one of the blueberries.

These two pieces of toast were carefully layered on top of each other, allowing the blueberries and syrup to easily rest on top without falling off.

Breakfast is, by far, my favorite meal of the day, so I tend to photograph variations of different breakfast meals often. One that is quite tasty, a classic rendition of French toast, also happens to be photogenic. The texture of the blueberries, warmth of the bread, and glossiness of the pouring syrup all combine to make a picture-perfect, sweet-and-delicious way to start the morning.

Canon 5D Mark III •
ISO 400 • 1/125 sec. •
ƒ/5.6 • Canon 100mm
ƒ/2.8L Macro lens

I repeated the blue color of the blueberries with the light blue fabric below the plate.

Poring Over the Picture

While I do consider myself a good cook, I will sometimes cheat in my photographs with a store-bought item. For this image of a birthday cupcake, the cakes were bought, and I added the frosting and sprinkles specifically for the photograph. Then, I placed a lit candle on top to complete the scene.

I dropped sprinkles throughout the scene to add a "messiness" and depth to the image.

I focused the lens on the large sprinkles in the front cupcake and used a large aperture to blur the background.

Canon 5D Mark III •
ISO 100 • 0.7 sec. •
ƒ/5.6 • Canon 100mm
ƒ/2.8L Macro lens

Types of Light

The great thing about lighting food for still photography is that a basic, simple lighting setup will create amazing results. You don't need a bunch of fancy or expensive equipment or an elaborate lighting setup to create your photographs. Often, just one light is all you need to beautifully light a mouthwatering plate of food.

Natural Light

Sunlight is, hands down, my favorite light source when photographing food. It's soft, natural, clean, bright, free, and easy to use. I use natural light as much as I can. It really fits my style of food photography well, and I love its simplicity (**Figure 2.1**). I do the majority of my food photography in my office and use a window that creates beautiful soft light. Also, using sunlight keeps my small space less cluttered than when I'm using larger studio lights.

If you want to try using this type of light, find a window with indirect, diffused light coming in. By diffused, I mean light that is not brightly shining in through the window. You'll basically want to stay away from harsh sunbeams shining in on your food.

As with everything, there are limitations to using natural sunlight. First, you can take advantage of it only during certain hours of the day, which can be inconvenient if you work a day job and come home just before the sun goes down. Another inconvenience is that even though there might be a lot of light coming in to light your food, there may not be enough for you to handhold your camera, depending on your settings. I find that with the camera setup I typically use (my lens set to f/8 at ISO 100), when photographing with window light, my shutter speed is slow enough that I always have to use a tripod.

Artificial Light

Although I use a lot of natural light with my food (mostly because it's easy and I have a nice setup), I do from time to time use studio lights (**Figure 2.2**). What's great about photographing with artificial light is that it allows you a lot of flexibility in regard to when and where you create your photographs. When you use sunlight, you obviously have to create your photos sometime during the day in a location that has good-quality, diffused sunlight, and you also will probably have to use a tripod. With strobe lights, you have complete control of when and where you create your photographs, which at times can be a necessity. Also, because you can usually use a faster shutter speed with strobes, you have the flexibility of handholding your camera, which can be especially useful if you like to experiment with different angles and compositions.

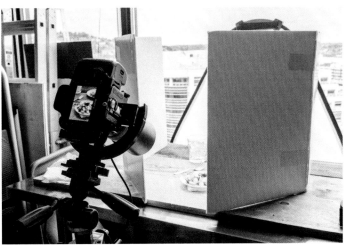

Figure 2.1
This is a standard setup that I use often: diffused, backlit window light with white foam board to bounce light back in to the scene.

Canon 5D Mark III · ISO 100 · 1/45 sec. · f/8 ·
Canon 100mm f/2.8L Macro lens

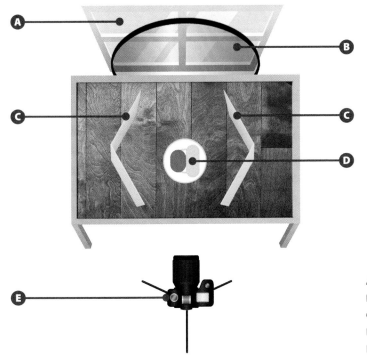

A Window light
B Diffusion Panel
C White foam board
D Caprese salad
E Canon 5D Mark III

Figure 2.2

When setting up a strobe for food photography, it is always my intention to re-create the look of natural light as much as possible.

Canon 5D Mark III • ISO 100 • 1/125 sec. • *f*/8 • Canon 100mm *f*/2.8L Macro lens

A AlienBees B800 Strobe
B Large rectangular softbox
C White foam board
D Caprese salad
E Canon 5D Mark III

There are two basic types of strobe lights: small flashes (**Figure 2.3**) and studio lights (**Figure 2.4**). My preference is for studio lights, mostly because I'm more familiar with them and I always have them readily available. I also prefer their broader options of modifiers (such as softboxes) that you can attach to diffuse the light. With that said, small flashes can be just as powerful and can create a similar quality of light to a studio strobe. They are also portable and lightweight, and because they use batteries, you don't have to search for an outlet, making them useful when photographing outdoors or on location.

If you don't have access to studio lights or diffused window sunlight, another option is to use a continuous light. Continuous lights are easy to use in the sense that they are a WYSIWYG (what you see is what you get) type of light. You can watch where the light falls on your subject, and you can also easily determine where to place other accessories, such as reflectors, to fill in the shadows.

Figure 2.3
Small flashes are a good choice when working on location because they are light and portable.

Figure 2.4
A strobe light, such as this AlienBees B800 strobe (www.paulcbuff.com), is a good option when you don't have enough available light in your scene.

Sync Speed

When using any type of strobe light (studio or small flash), you need to keep in mind that its sync speed (the speed in which the light can synchronize with the shutter speed) is limited to a maximum of about 1/250 of a second (this number may differ depending on the brand and model of your camera). Don't set your camera's shutter speed to be faster than this sync speed. If you were to accidentally set it too fast, either you would get an underexposed image or most of your photo would be black.

When using continuous lights, keep in mind that they can get hot, which could potentially heat up the food you're photographing. Even if your food is hot to begin with, the plate will likely contain some items, such as fresh herbs or garnishes, which will start to look bad when they get warm. The heat from the light will rapidly spoil the look of the food, so you'll need to work quickly to get a fresh-looking food photograph.

Another thing to consider is the color of light created by continuous lights. If you can find a daylight-balanced light, your chances of producing an image with proper color balance are much greater than if you use fluorescent or tungsten light bulbs.

Lighting Modifiers and Accessories

Whether you're using sunlight or strobes, you'll probably need a few extra items, such as reflectors, softboxes, or umbrellas, to help light up your image. With food photography, it's easy to keep things simple; you don't have to go overboard with accessories and gear to get a great photograph. Keep on reading to learn about some useful tools you can use with your food photography.

Figure 2.5
The Lastolite Tri-Grip reflector (www.lastolite.com) is a great choice for food photographers because you can either easily prop it up on a table (without it rolling away) or hold it with one hand while triggering the shutter with the other.

Reflectors

If you had to choose only one accessory to use when photographing food, I highly recommend a reflector (Figure 2.5). Reflectors are basically anything that will reflect light. In photography, reflectors are used primarily as fill lights to fill in areas that look dark or overly shaded.

When you are photographing food and backlighting your subject, you'll probably place a reflector or two in the front of the image. Just like with any type of light, the closer your reflector is to your subject, the brighter it will be, and the larger your reflector is, the softer the light will be. Also, the color of your reflector is extremely important because that color will reflect back onto your subject. I recommend using a silver or white reflector to ensure that you don't add any strange colorcasts to your photograph.

The great thing about reflectors is that they don't have to be fancy or expensive. I use a lot of standard photographic reflectors with my food photography, but I also find that simply using large rectangles of white foam board, which you can find at any craft store, is an effective way to fill in the shadows with a nice, soft light. What I like to do is to cut the piece of foam board in half and tape it back together to form a sort of bookend that can be propped up on its own next to the food (**Figure 2.6**).

Diffusers

Another important tool in my food photography arsenal is a diffuser. The job of a diffuser is to soften the source of the light, which would be either a strobe, a flash, or even the light coming through a window. One basic rule to remember with light and diffusers, especially when working with strobes and flashes, is that the *bigger* the light source and the *closer* the light is to your subject, the *softer* the light will be. And using a modifier, such as a softbox or umbrella, will help *increase* the size of your light.

The following sections highlight several of the different types of diffusers you can use with your photography.

Diffusion Panels

A diffusion panel is a large piece of fabric that you can place between the light source and your subject to soften the intensity of the light. They come in different sizes, ranging from handheld to several feet tall. When using window light, I typically use one large panel in front of the window (4 by 6 feet), and if the light is still too bright, I will supplement it with smaller triangle-shaped diffusers (**Figure 2.7**).

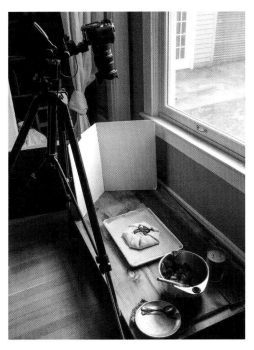

Figure 2.6
In this example, I am using one folded piece of white foam board to bounce light back onto the food.

Figure 2.7
This 4-by-6-foot diffusion panel is almost always propped up against the window behind my food photography table.

Figure 2.8
Softboxes come in many shapes and sizes; the larger the softbox, the more light that it will diffuse.

Figure 2.9
This is a shoot-through umbrella; the light goes through the white, translucent umbrella, diffusing before it reaches the subject.

Softboxes

If you decide you want to use studio lights or even small flashes for your food photography, I highly recommend adding a softbox to your inventory of photography equipment (**Figure 2.8**). Softboxes diffuse the light so that it's soft and can wrap around your subject. They are a must if your goal is to minimize the harsh shadows in your photographs.

Umbrellas

If you don't have a softbox, another good alternative would be to use an umbrella (**Figure 2.9**). There are two basic types of umbrellas: reflective and shoot-through. A *reflective* umbrella is angled so that the strobe is firing into the umbrella and the light bounces back onto the subject. The *shoot-through* variety is set up so that the strobe fires through an umbrella made of white, translucent material.

Quality of Light

All light is not the same. The light you see in the middle of the day looks different when compared to the warm sunlight that shines an hour before sunset. The light coming from the fluorescent light bulb in your kitchen is not the same as the light coming from the tungsten light bulb on your nightstand. Different light sources create different colors, intensities, and moods.

Now, this doesn't mean that one type of light is better than another, but it may be true that certain light sources are better for certain types of photography. For portrait and landscape photography, the first hour and last hour of sunset are ideal times to create images outdoors, and studio photographers have ways of manipulating light with strobes to add drama or softness to their images. Each of these types of light creates a different mood, which is often referred to as the *quality* of the light.

Color

The color of light you use with food photography is extremely important. My advice is to stick with light that is daylight balanced, like sunlight or strobes. If the color is off, it's likely that the orange-reddish cast from, let's say, a tungsten light source will remain, and a strange or unusual color cast on a food photograph is just not appetizing (**Figure 2.10**). Using the most beautiful (and appropriate) quality of light coupled with a proper white balance will ensure that the color of your photographs looks its best (**Figure 2.11**).

Figure 2.10
This image was photographed in the yellowish overhead light inside my office.

Canon 5D Mark III · ISO 100 · 1.5 sec. · f/5.6 ·
Canon 100mm f/2.8L Macro lens

Figure 2.11
For this photo, I turned off the overhead lights and used only the light coming from the window.

Canon 5D Mark III · ISO 100 · 0.7 sec. · f/5.6 ·
Canon 100mm f/2.8L Macro lens

When it comes to the color of light, keep in mind that you want only one type of light in your photo. For example, if you're using a window to light your food but you have another light nearby that's bright—enough to "contaminate" the light in the photograph—then you might get some funky colors going on that will be difficult to correct. It's usually a good idea to get into the habit of turning off all the light switches in your room before photographing your food.

Intensity

When selecting a light source for your food images, be sure to consider the intensity of the light you're using. Some light sources are stronger than others, and it's important to know how to work with the light you're using.

If you're photographing with diffused sunlight, you won't really need to worry about the intensity of the light because the light is likely pretty soft. You will need to be aware of this, however, when using studio (strobe) lights. If you go for the biggest, baddest, and most powerful light you can find, you might realize that it's *too* powerful if you are planning to use a wide aperture to blur your background. Strobe lights have a maximum shutter speed they can be set to (maxing out at around 1/250 of a second). If the light is too strong at its lowest setting (and you're already set to ISO 100), then the only other setting you can change is your aperture. If your goal is to blur your background, you won't want to use an f-stop that is too small.

If you do happen to have a light that is too powerful, you can soften it so that it works better for your food photographs. One way is to diffuse the light with a light modifier, such as a softbox or shoot-through umbrella, or by placing any type of white translucent substance in front of the light source. If you happen to have a window that has only harsh sunlight coming through, you could try covering the window with something like white translucent vellum paper, or you could use a *scrim*, which is basically just a piece of translucent fabric, to soften and block the harsh rays of the sun.

Distance

The location and distance of the light in relation to your subject will play a huge part in determining the softness or harshness of the light. One basic principle is that the bigger and closer the light is to your subject, the softer the light will be. If you want soft shadows, you can make your light bigger by attaching modifiers, such as softboxes and shoot-through umbrellas, to diffuse the light source. Then, once you have a nice big light by bringing it close to your subject, you get a soft light with few shadows.

The best way to understand this is to think of the sun. True, the sun is a really, really big light source, but it's also *very* far away. Imagine it's a sunny day at 1 p.m. and you're standing outside on the sidewalk. You look down at your shadow, and what do you see? A nice, crisp, dark shadow, right? Now picture that same scene but with an overcast sky. What does your shadow look like now? If there is one at all, it's probably faded and soft, but it's also possible that your shadow is gone. Those clouds basically made the sky into a giant softbox and diffused the light.

This is an extremely important concept to understand. If you want soft light with minimal shadows, you'll want to get the light as close to your subject as possible, and you can still turn down the intensity of the light to balance the exposure. If you're going for harsh shadows and intense, moody light, then all you have to do is move the light farther away from your subject.

Direction of Light

Another thing to consider when setting up your lights for food photography is where you want the light to actually come from. The goal with lighting any photograph is to light the image in a pleasing way so that you enhance the subject matter. In this section, I will discuss three types of light: backlight, sidelight, and frontlight, along with their advantages (and, in some cases, disadvantages).

Backlight

Most food photographers agree that the best light for food photography is backlight. The concept is quite simple, really. To get a pleasing backlit look, place the light directly behind your subject. I prefer this light when I am photographing the food at eye-level (**Figure 2.12**).

Backlight adds texture and depth to an image, and (my favorite) it rim-lights your subject and brightens up certain food items such as mint leaves or slices of citrus. Keep in mind that while it's sometimes nice to keep your light soft, having shadows in your photo isn't necessarily a bad thing. Don't be afraid of a little bit of contrast; just make sure you are constantly aware of how the light is affecting your subject.

Figure 2.12
Backlighting a scene adds a lot of brightness to the background, which typically needs to be compensated with reflectors. It is a beautiful option for many food setups, however, and can add rim-light and glow to certain ingredients, such as herbs and citrus slices.

Canon 5D Mark III · ISO 100 · 1/10 sec. · ƒ/4 · Canon 100mm ƒ/2.8L Macro lens

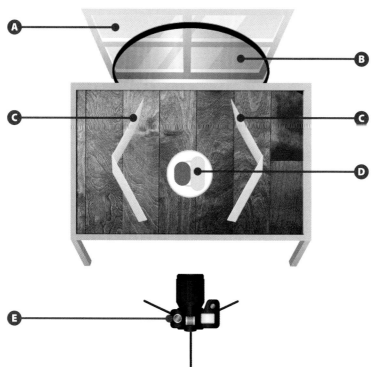

A Window light
B Diffusion panel
C White foam board
D Tea and
   macaroons
E Canon 5D Mark III

Sidelight

Another really good option for food photography is sidelight (**Figure 2.13**). Sidelight will help add depth and shadows to an image, and it works well with food that has a reflective surface, such as soup or beverages. This lighting setup is a good choice if you want more control over the shadows in your images, particularly if you want to intensify the shadows (**Figures 2.14** and **2.15**).

Figure 2.13
Sidelight is another wonderful option for photographing food. It is also a simple setup that may or may not require the use of a reflector.

Canon 5D Mark III · ISO 100 · 1/20 sec. · ƒ/4 · Canon 100mm ƒ/2.8L Macro lens

A Window light
B Diffusion panel
C Tea and macaroons
D White foam board
E Canon 5D Mark III

Figure 2.14
For this image, I placed a reflector to the left to fill in the shadows.

Canon 5D Mark III • ISO 100 • 1/15 sec. • ƒ/4 • Canon 100mm ƒ/2.8L Macro lens

A Window light
B Diffusion panel
C Tea and macaroons
D White foam board
E Canon 5D Mark III

Figure 2.15
I removed the reflector to intensify the shadows for this frame.
....
Canon 5D Mark III · ISO 100 · 1/10 sec. · ƒ/4 · Canon 100mm ƒ/2.8L Macro lens

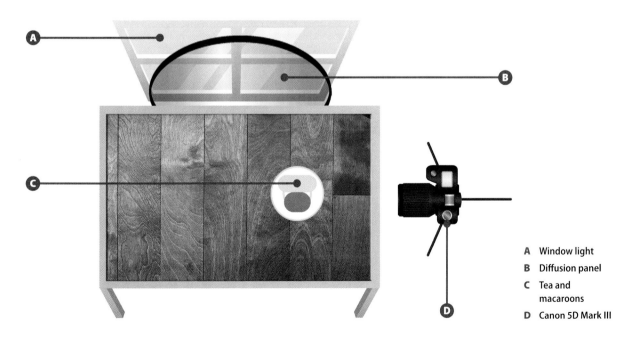

A Window light
B Diffusion panel
C Tea and macaroons
D Canon 5D Mark III

Frontlight

Frontlight for food is not necessarily a bad thing, so long as you are using a pleasing light source. I would probably not set up a photograph at home using this type of light, but if I am photographing my meal at a restaurant, frontlight can oftentimes be the best way to go (**Figure 2.16**).

One downfall to using frontlight is that you will tend to end up with a much darker background (**Figure 2.17**). Because you are metering for the food, which is likely the brightest portion of your image in the front of the scene, the rest of the image will be much darker. You can bring some of this light back with reflectors and fill cards (simple white pieces of foam board), but it's not going to look as natural as if you were lighting the food from a different direction.

Overall, you will want to choose the direction of light that suits your preference, style, and what best enhances the dish you are photographing. Try various lighting setups, and pay attention to how they affect your images. One setup will not be best for all images. Regardless of which direction the light is coming from, watch how it's affecting *everything* in your photograph, such as the background, flatware, and reflections.

Figure 2.16
When I feel like photographing my food at a restaurant, frontlight is sometimes the best light for the job.

Fuji X-T1 · ISO 6400 · 1/35 sec · ƒ/5.6 · Zeiss 32mm ƒ/1.8 lens

Figure 2.17
Frontlight does a good job of lighting the subject, but it loses the depth and shadow details that you get when the light is coming from another angle.
....
Canon 5D Mark III · ISO 100 · 1/15 sec. · ƒ/4 · Canon 100mm ƒ/2.8L Macro lens

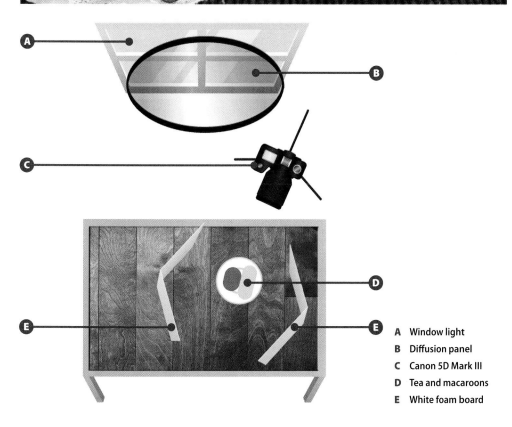

A   Window light
B   Diffusion panel
C   Canon 5D Mark III
D   Tea and macaroons
E   White foam board

Backlight

Sidelight

Frontlight

Chapter 2 Challenges

Now that you're familiar with many different ways to light your food photographs, here are a few lighting challenges to try on your own.

Play with the Angles of Light

Prepare a dish to photograph, and set it up similarly to the way I demonstrated the angles of light in this chapter: backlight, sidelight, and frontlight. Photograph the dish with each of these three setups, and compare them to see which one is the most complementary to the food.

Use a Reflector

Place an item near a window with diffused natural light, and arrange it so that your subject is sidelit with the light from the window. Take a look at your scene, paying careful attention to the amount of shadow on the side of your subject. Just use your eyes; you don't need a camera for this first part. Next, place a reflector (or a large piece of white foam board) on the side opposite the window. Move it back and forth, and watch how it fills in the shadows in the front.

Grab your camera, and photograph the scene with a balanced exposure and your camera mode set to Manual. First, take a photo without using the reflector. Take another photo without changing your settings, but this time use the reflector to fill in the sides and front of your subject. Compare the images on your LCD monitor, watching how the light comes and goes and how adding a reflector can help brighten up the shadows.

Experiment with Diffusers and Modifiers

Set up a dish to photograph, and have a few different methods of diffusing the light on hand. If you are using natural light, try photographing the food with and without a diffusion panel to see how the light and shadows compare between each shot. If you are using a strobe or flash, do the same (with and without a diffuser, such as a softbox or umbrella). Notice how the shadows become softer the more you diffuse the light.

Share your results with the book's Flickr group! Join the group here: flickr.com/groups/ foodphotographyfromsnapshotstogreatshots

Canon 5D Mark III •
ISO 100 • 1/20 sec. •
ƒ/4 • Canon 100mm
ƒ/2.8L Macro lens

3
Styling and Props

The Art of Presentation

One of the reasons I love food photography is that I truly enjoy styling and crafting the food, and one of the biggest compliments I get from people is that my images made them hungry! When we eat food, all of our senses are at work—we see, smell, touch, and taste the food—but when we look at a photo, we can use our eyes only. Styling food is one way to capture its flavors, aromas, and textures and to communicate them to viewers. Creating an amazing-looking dish is an art, whether you eat it or photograph it, and you can do a lot of little things to enhance the look of the food and (ideally) make people salivate when they view your photographs.

Poring Over the Picture

I added a small plate with a wooden spoon in the background to balance out the scene.

On a trip to Thailand, I discovered a new favorite dish: Khao Soi. It's a spicy, curried noodle dish with tons of spices and aromatics that is traditionally topped with fried noodles. When I got home, I wanted to make the recipe a little bit healthier. So instead of adding fried noodles to the top, I added a handful of micro greens. Not only do they make the dish healthier, they also make it more colorful!

Canon 5D Mark III · ISO 100 · 0.5 sec. · f/5.6 · Canon 100mm f/2.8L Macro lens

I used a very small bowl to make the elements inside of the bowl look larger.

A piece of white foam board bounces light back in to the side of the dish.

Poring Over the Picture

One thing I love to photograph is any type of pancake or French toast. There is a lot of potential for color, style, and texture, and I find myself photographing (and eating) them quite often! These little pancakes were made with coconut flour, filled with yogurt, and topped with blueberries and huckleberries. The berries add a nice touch of sweetness and color to a healthy breakfast.

I photographed this at eye level to add height to the pancakes.

Canon 5D Mark III •
ISO 100 • 1/45 sec. •
f/5.6 • Canon 100mm
f/2.8L Macro lens

A small sprig of mint placed on top adds color.

I used white plates and a light tabletop surface to highlight the colors of the food.

Styling Considerations

When we photograph our food, we want it to look beautiful, mouth-watering, and delicious. But there are several issues to consider before you go full speed.

Using a Food Stylist

Food stylists are extremely talented artists, most often with a culinary background. Their job is to make food look fresh and appetizing for the camera, so an understanding of how food acts and behaves is a must. They know all the tricks and techniques to create beautiful-looking dishes and use their skills to make the food look as delicious as it tastes. Does every food photographer need to work with a food stylist? It depends.

If you are the photographer for a big production (one with a large budget or for a high-profile company), having a stylist is a good idea. Even if you have the chops to style the food yourself, doing both the photography and the styling would probably be overwhelming. Hiring a food stylist ensures that your main focus stays where it should be: creating the photographs. Styling food on set is a one- or maybe two-person job, so when you are in an environment where time is limited (or there are several food items to style and photograph), then you are probably better off working with a professional food stylist.

On the other hand, if you're a food blogger or you just want to photograph food for fun, then it's likely you don't have the budget to hire a bona-fide food stylist. In that case, it's up to you to learn how to style your food and present it so that it not only looks appetizing but also looks good on camera. Later in this chapter I will show you some of my favorite tools and techniques that you can use to make food look beautiful all on your own.

Ethical Considerations

When it comes to styling food, there are some ethical restrictions that you must adhere to, mostly when you're photographing food for commercial purposes. The basic guideline is that if you're photographing food for advertisements (such as an ice cream image for a specific brand of ice cream), then you need to photograph the actual product, which in this case would be ice cream. If the advertisement is for a particular brand of ice cream, then you can't photograph fake ice cream and pass it off as the real thing.

But let's say you are hired to photograph sprinkles and toppings that go on top of the ice cream. In this case, the product that is being advertised is *not* the ice cream itself, so you could use fake ice cream because ice cream is, after all, one of the more difficult things to style and photograph. With all that said, I am not a lawyer, so if you find yourself in an unclear situation, it's best to do your own research and also seek legal advice if necessary.

Styled Food vs. Real Food

When you see an advertisement with a photograph of a fast-food hamburger, odds are that a food stylist had a heavy hand in making that hamburger look as juicy, plump, and deliciously messy as it could possibly be. If you go through the drive-through and order that same hamburger, however, you're likely going to be underwhelmed by the looks of the actual food that you receive. Although the beautiful hamburger in the photograph may in fact have been "real" food (with some added stylistic effects), it sure as heck was not *realistic*.

So what exactly is food styling? If you ask me, it has a broad range of definitions. Some people may consider food styling to encompass only the "weird" things that can be done to enhance the look of food, such as using aerosol starch and motor oil on pancakes, or soap bubbles in coffee or on bacon. The reason those types of styling options are popular is because they photograph well, look realistic, and also have a longer shelf life on set. My own definition is much more liberal because I think that we all style our food. Every intentional adjustment you make to your dishes, whether it's for food you're going to eat or to photograph, is styling. When chefs prepare meals at restaurants, they also style their dishes. Presentation is extremely important with food, especially when it's going to be photographed; when you can't smell the food, hear it sizzle, or hold it in your hands, its appearance is everything (**Figures 3.1** and **3.2**).

Figure 3.1
These images show how using something as simple as a cookie cutter to refine the edges of a small cheesecake can make a huge difference in its appearance. The integrity of the food was not compromised in styling this dish; rather, it was just prepared carefully so that it looked more elegant for the camera.

Photographed with an iPhone 6+

Figure 3.2
To style this dish, I used a cookie cutter to shape the cheesecake and then topped it with pomegranates and candied lemon peel.

Canon 5D Mark III •
ISO 100 • 2 sec. •
ƒ/5.6 • Canon 100mm
ƒ/2.8L Macro lens

You see, styling food doesn't mean you need to compromise the integrity of the dish and contaminate it with nonfood items in order to create a stunning photograph. To me, nothing is more beautiful than real food, but it still takes a bit of work to make that food look good for a photograph. You can also create your entire dish and do a bit of "editing" to the plate, which can be as basic as taking what is in front of you and moving things around to make it look more appealing.

The way you style and present your food is up to you, and the ultimate purpose of your photograph will also play a role in the presentation. If you run a website that showcases recipes and food, you might want to make your dish look as real as possible and only edit or style it to represent the recipe both truthfully and attractively. Or, if you just love food and want to create beautiful dishes for the love of photography, sneaking in a few "tricks" may not be such a bad thing. There's no right or wrong way to style food; just do what fits the purpose of your photography and your own personal style.

Ensuring Food Quality

When you cook a meal, you want to use quality ingredients to get the best flavors possible, right? When photographing food, you want to make sure that you follow the same principle, while ensuring that the way each ingredient *looks* is just as important as its *flavor*. It's simple, really—find only the most beautiful food to photograph.

Using Fresh Ingredients

The key to achieving a high-quality look for the food in your photographs is to use the freshest ingredients possible. Food doesn't last forever, and its beauty usually dissipates before it spoils or loses flavor. Herbs and veggies sitting in a refrigerator have a limited life span, so make sure you plan your photographs in advance and try to buy your food *the day* or *the day before* it's photographed.

To ensure that the quality of my food is up to par, I tend to shop only at certain grocery stores and markets. I know that some locations will have, for example, a really great selection of seafood, so I go to one of those stores when I'm shopping for that ingredient. I also like to go to the local farmers market to buy seasonal produce and fruit, and sometimes I'll conceive the look of a dish based on the freshest ingredients I can find while I'm shopping.

I also prefer to use fresh food rather than canned food, especially when it comes to vegetables (I will, from time to time, use frozen vegetables because they hold their shape and color well after being cooked). The guideline I use is that if I can buy it fresh (in the produce section of the grocery store), then I stay away from any canned alternatives. This also gives me a lot more control over the shape, color, size, and texture of the food. I make exceptions to this, of course, such as when I want to use something like canned mandarin oranges or water chestnuts. The bottom line is that if the food looks good enough to photograph, whether it's fresh or comes out of the can, bag, or jar, then go ahead and use it.

Shopping Smartly

When purchasing the ingredients for your dish, you need to be extremely selective. Choosing the most attractive ingredients (also referred to as the *hero* food) is essential to a great-looking dish. It's also a good idea to buy more than you need. (You can always eat the leftovers!) Having more than one of each item gives you options for the look of the ingredient, and it's also insurance in case anything goes wrong with your first pick.

When shopping for ingredients, be aware of how they will be handled when they are scanned at the register. If you have a self-checkout lane, then that's a good option if you are purchasing something fragile or easily altered, such as bread or soft fruit. Otherwise, kindly let the clerk know that you are photographing the food and ask if they can handle it with care. Another option is to find a discarded cardboard box and place the items in there so that they are not unintentionally squished at the bottom of a grocery bag. One of my favorite places to shop for produce is the local farmer's market (**Figure 3.3**). Not only is the food beautiful, I get to do all of the handling myself!

I am also very selective about the ingredients that I choose for my photographs. If I have one particular ingredient that will stand out, such as an artichoke, then I will search through all of the artichokes until I find a few of them that have the right shape and color for the image I want to create. If I am purchasing something in the meat department, I will usually ask for a specific item and will also ask the butcher to handle it with care because I will be photographing it. And, if you don't find what you are looking for, then either find a different ingredient or go to another store. Never compromise the look of an ingredient if you don't have to.

Figure 3.3
I prefer to shop for produce at the local farmer's market. The produce is fresh, and it's easy to find beautiful items to cook with.
Fuji X-T1 · ISO 400 · 1/800 sec. · ƒ/2.8 · Zeiss Touit 50mm ƒ/2.8

Food Styling Basics

There is no single right (or wrong) way to style food, but there are some things that many food stylists and photographers do to make the food look its best. Before I get into the how, I'll start with the what. For instance, **Figure 3.4** shows some of the gadgets and tools that I use (and you can use) to make it all happen.

Gadgets and Tools

I use a lot of little gadgets and tools when styling food, but many of them are just everyday kitchen utensils. Here is a list of some of the basic tools I use often and wouldn't want to be without:

Figure 3.4
This is a sampling of some of the tools I use when styling food.

Canon 5D Mark III · ISO 400 · 1/10 sec. · ƒ/6.7 · Canon 100mm ƒ/2.8L Macro lens

- **Tweezers**: I use tweezers to place small items (such as mint leaves or sesame seeds) or to reposition things on the plate.

- **Prep bowls and ramekins**: These are really useful for holding garnishes and sauces near your dish or workspace. You can also place them upside down in bowls to add bulk to foods.

- **Plastic spoons**: These are useful for mixing and stirring, as well as for applying things such as sauces, sour cream, or any kind of liquid. Because they are extremely light and thin, I find that they give me more control than metal spoons.

- **Paper towels**: I always have a full roll of paper towels sitting near my workspace when styling food. They're handy for cleaning drips on plates, and if you're styling food in the spot where it will be photographed, you can place them under the plate to catch accidental spills.

- **Water**: I use canned water to add a fine mist to salad, fresh fruits and vegetables, and the like.

- **Grater and peeler**: These are great for preparing garnishes, such as Parmesan cheese or lemon zest.

Using Stand-ins

If you're familiar with movie or television production, you know that the lights need to be set for each scene, which usually takes quite a while. So, instead of having the main actors sit or stand on the set while the lights are being moved and measured, *stand-ins* (people who have a similar look to the actors) take their place so the actors can relax, have their makeup fixed, memorize their lines, or simply stay in character. A similar method is used in food photography.

When you style and photograph food, you usually have to work quickly so the food stays fresh. All food has a limited life span, which is even more apparent when you're photographing it. Shiny food loses its luster, oils and sauces soak into cooked meats, and foods such as herbs and lettuce wilt away quickly (**Figure 3.5**).

When I photograph food, I always use a stand-in. I do this so I can set the lights, composition, props, and so on, ahead of time and prevent the food from losing its luster by the time everything is ready to go. In fact, I don't even do any cooking, styling, or preparations until the light is ready. That way, once the food is prepared, I can drop it into place, make a few minor adjustments, and start photographing within seconds of the food being placed on set.

A stand-in can be anything. An extra piece of food that doesn't require cooking (such as a hamburger bun) usually makes a good stand-in. Or you could use something totally random that has similar tonal qualities as your prepared food will have (**Figures 3.6** and **3.7**). Try to use something that is the same shape, width, or height so you can set your composition in the camera (this is especially handy if you are using a tripod).

Figure 3.5
This sequence shows how much a simple herb such as basil can change over the course of one hour—it goes from being crisp and green to dull and wilting.

Canon 5D Mark III · ISO 50 · 1/6 sec. · ƒ/6.7 · Canon 24–70mm ƒ/2.8L lens

Canon 5D Mark III ·
ISO 100 · 1/4 sec. ·
f/5.6 · Canon 100mm
f/2.8L Macro lens

Canon 5D Mark III ·
ISO 100 · 0.3 sec. ·
f/5.6 · Canon 100mm
f/2.8L Macro lens

Figure 3.6
I used a crumpled-up napkin as a stand-in for the yogurt in this photograph.

Canon 5D Mark III ·
ISO 100 · 0.3 sec. ·
f/6.7 · Canon 100mm
f/2.8L Macro lens

Canon 5D Mark III ·
ISO 100 · 0.7 sec. ·
f/6.7 · Canon 100mm
f/2.8L Macro len

Figure 3.7
A stand-in doesn't need to look identical to your actual food. In this case, I placed a simple knitted cloth on the plate as a stand-in for the pasta.

Maintaining a Clean Environment

A perfectly prepared photo setup can easily be tainted with an unwanted stain. When I'm preparing a plate of food for a photograph, therefore, I try to do most of the work away from the location where it will be photographed, usually on my kitchen counter or at a table that sits nearby. This way I can get close to the dish as well as keep all my tools, food, and garnishes nearby, and it doesn't matter if I make a mess.

Sometimes, however, you won't be able to do all of your plating off set and will need to style the dish as it sits in front of the camera. In those instances, you need to be careful to protect the environment from drips and spills. The simplest solution is to place a few paper towels around the area (**Figure 3.8**), which will likely save you from having to quickly re-create your scene. This also allows you to focus on the look of the food without worrying about making any messes.

Styling from Camera View

When photographing food, the only area of the food that you need to pay attention to is the side that's being photographed. It's always best to put yourself in the position of the camera and style the food from that perspective. If you're photographing the front part of a dish, it doesn't matter what the back of the dish looks like, so long as it's not in the image.

Another useful way to style food (and set up the overall scene, too) is to use the Live View feature on your camera (most of the newer DSLR models have this as a standard feature). Being able to watch what is happening in your scene with Live View makes it so easy to place things in the scene, add garnishes, and even just frame and compose the photo. The downside to Live View is that it drains the battery more quickly than just looking through the viewfinder. It also will sometimes cause interference when you're firing strobes and flashes wirelessly. If you run into that problem, you'll need to turn off Live View temporarily to trip the shutter and create the photograph.

Following Your Instincts

Overall, much of styling food involves using what works for your situation. There is no one way to do everything, and depending on how the food was prepared or how you want it to look, you'll probably have to get creative.

You also need to make sure that you are deliberate in your approach to creating your food and developing its overall appearance. When I style food, everything that ends up in the photograph is there because I want it to be there. A crumb that looks like it landed naturally on the plate may have been placed with small tweezers, or it crumbled off on its own and I just liked the way it landed. Often it's the things that may be considered small and unimportant that can actually take a photo from average to amazing.

Figure 3.8
When working with messy food, such as this berry bruschetta topping, place paper towels over the table's surface to prevent drips and stains.

Canon 5D Mark III • ISO 100 • 1/4 sec. • ƒ/6.7 • Canon 100mm ƒ/2.8L Macro lens

Figure 3.9
By placing a small upside-down cup in the bowl, I was able to "float" the asparagus tips on the top of the soup. Without the small cup, they would have sunk to the bottom of the soup bowl.

Canon 60D · ISO 100 · 1/20 sec. · *f*/2 · Canon 50mm *f*/1.4 lens

Canon 60D · ISO 100 · 1/20 sec. · *f*/2 · Canon 50mm *f*/1.4 lens

Styling Tips and Tricks

There are a lot of techniques you can use when styling your food to enhance its appearance. Here are some simple tips and tricks to help you make your food look great when it's being photographed.

Adding Bulk

When you place food in a bowl, often it will sink to the bottom and lie flat (especially with foods like pasta and chunky soups or stews). You can bulk up food in a bowl in a few ways. The first is to set a dome of Styrofoam in the bottom of the bowl and then place the food on top of it. This usually works best for slippery foods that won't stay put, but one major downside is that if you're planning to eat the food after it's photographed, you're out of luck (unless you want little bits of plastic foam in your meal). Another

Canon 60D · ISO 100 ·
1/30 sec. · ƒ/2 ·
Canon 50mm ƒ/1.4 lens

Canon 60D · ISO 100 ·
1/10 sec. · ƒ/2.5 ·
Canon 50mm ƒ/1.4 lens

method is to place a smaller bowl, such as a prep dish or small ramekin, upside down in the bowl and then pile the food on top (**Figure 3.9**). This keeps your food fresh and does a really good job of adding a little extra bulk. For soups, another good trick is to use clear glass stones at the bottom of the bowl to help bring any added items up to the surface, such as noodles or vegetables.

If you're working with food that is flat, especially when you are stacking more than one item on top of the other, adding something between the layers can help make the food look much more full. In **Figure 3.10**, I placed two tortillas on top of each other before adding the carnitas meat and garnish. However, just having the tortillas lie flat on top of each other made them look lifeless. So I added torn-up tortillas between the layers to help bring up the front edges and make them look more appealing. You can use anything you like between your food to give it more life—cardboard, toothpicks, or even folded-up paper towels.

Figure 3.10

I added torn-up tortilla pieces between the two tortillas to add bulk and texture to the food.

Canon 5D Mark III · ISO 100 · 0.5 sec. · *f*/5.6 · Canon 100mm *f*/2.8L Macro lens

Using Garnishes

Adding a touch of color to a dish can do wonders, and I often do this by adding garnishes, such as fresh basil, cilantro, or any herb that is appropriate to the food and its ingredients (**Figure 3.11**). Just as adding herbs and spices will enhance flavor when cooking the food, adding them to your photograph can make it look livelier and more appealing.

This technique also helps create your point of focus. By adding a bright, colorful food item to the dish, you will draw the viewer's eyes to that location. And it's the perfect spot to focus on with your camera. (Chapter 5 offers more suggestions on focus and composition.)

Canon 5D Mark III · ISO 100 · 1/6 sec. · ƒ/8 · Canon 100mm ƒ/2.8L Macro lens

Canon 5D Mark III · ISO 100 · 1/4 sec. · ƒ/8 · Canon 100mm ƒ/2.8L Macro lens

Figure 3.11
Adding green onions and cilantro as a garnish helped give this photo a boost of color.

A Little Mess Is Okay

One thing to keep in mind when you're creating your dishes is that they don't always have to look perfect. A few crumbs or drips to the side of the food, or even a dish with a fork already dug into the food, makes the food look more real and attainable to the viewer (**Figure 3.12**). It can also add balance to the composition of the photograph. A little mess is okay; just pay attention to your crumb or drip placement so that it still looks appealing and delicious.

Figure 3.12
Adding a little bit of mess, like these drips coming off of the peaches, helps add realism to the photo.

Canon 5D Mark III · ISO 100 · 3 sec. · ƒ/5.6 · Canon 100mm ƒ/2.8L Macro lens

Real Ice vs. Fake Ice

Tip

When adding ice to a glass, be sure to fill it all the way up to the top so that the ice is peeking slightly above the liquid's surface. Real ice floats, but fake ice does not, so filling to the brim is a "sneaky" way to make it look more realistic!

I use fake ice in many of my photographs. In fact, any time there's a water glass in the frame (usually in the out-of-focus background), I've probably added some fake ice to the cup, usually without even adding water (**Figure 3.13**). I use fake ice so frequently because real ice has two major flaws: It melts quickly, and it can look very foggy when photographed. Fake ice, on the other hand, will hold its shape and stay shiny and crystal clear (**Figure 3.14**).

Figure 3.13
For this plate of pasta, I wanted to add something to the background. So I filled a glass with fake ice and placed it in the top left corner of the frame, knowing that it would end up blurred and slightly unrecognizable. The ice adds depth and a bit of sparkle to the background without being overpowering.

Canon 5D Mark III · ISO 100 · 0.7 sec. · ƒ/4.5 · Canon 100mm ƒ/2.8L Macro lens

Figure 3.14
These two images show the difference between fake ice (left) and real ice (right).

Canon 5D Mark III · ISO 100 · 1/10 sec. · ƒ/8 · Canon 100mm ƒ/2.8L Macro lens

Although there are places that create custom, realistic (and expensive) acrylic ice cubes, the ice I use is relatively inexpensive and purchased through an online retailer. If you are creating photographs that require ice and you don't have a big budget, this is probably a good option for you as well.

Adding Movement

Another way to add to your image is to give the photo a sense of movement. You could do this by photographing the act of drizzling syrup onto French toast, sprinkling cheese over pasta, or even adding a utensil that is taking a scoop from the food itself (**Figure 3.15**). One of my tricks for adding movement is to use a Manfrotto Magic Arm (www.manfrotto.com). By placing a spoon or fork in the jaws of this adjustable arm-like clamp I can mimic the act of someone taking a bite (**Figures 3.16** and **3.17**). The Magic Arm's flexibility allows me a lot of control when styling and framing my scene while keeping the utensil firmly in place (**Figure 3.18**).

Figure 3.15
Drizzling syrup over French toast is a great way to add movement to an image.

Canon 5D Mark III · ISO 400 · 1/125 sec. · ƒ/5.6 · Canon 100mm ƒ/2.8L Macro lens

Figure 3.16
I used a Manfrotto Magic Arm to set up this shot as if someone was holding a fork off camera.

Canon 5D Mark II • ISO 100 • 0.3 sec. • f/8 • Canon 70–200mm f/4L IS lens

Figure 3.17
The Manfrotto Magic Arm was used to create this image of honey dripping from a honey dipper.

Canon 5D Mark III • ISO 100 • 1/4 sec. • f/5.6 • Canon 100mm f/2.8L Macro lens

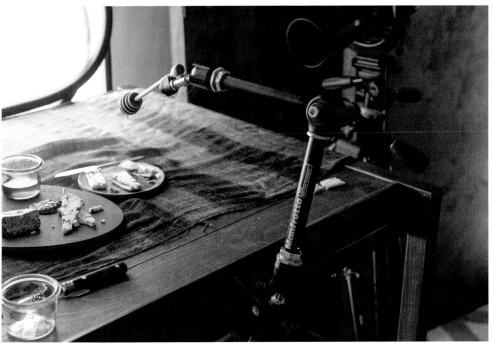

Figure 3.18
This is a behind-the-scenes image showing how the Manfrotto Magic Arm was positioned to create the image in Figure 3.17.

Fuji X-T1 • ISO 2500 • 1/125 sec. • f/3.6 • Zeiss Touit 32mm f/1.8 lens

Prop Styling

In really big food photography productions, along with a food stylist you're likely to find a prop stylist. This person is in charge of the plates, napkins, tablecloth, and anything else in the scene that is not food. If you're styling and photographing your own food, then this job falls on your shoulders. Don't neglect it because although it might not seem important at first, the props you use can really make or break a food photograph.

How you style the area around your food can greatly affect the mood and overall impression of the photograph. The props can suggest the location, time of day, season, and perhaps even who might be about to enjoy the meal (**Figure 3.19**). All of this can be achieved through the colors, textures, and shapes of your dishes, textiles, and props. The possibilities are endless.

Figure 3.19
I used barn wood as a tabletop surface to mimic the look of a picnic table.

Canon 5D Mark III • ISO 100 • 0.3 sec. • ƒ/5.6 • Canon 70–200mm ƒ/4L IS lens

Relevance and Simplicity

When adding props to a scene, imagine yourself sitting down at the table to eat the meal you are photographing. Picture the utensils, food, and dishes that might be set around you, things that you would actually use in real life. Then, take that information and apply it to your photograph.

Just remember, if it doesn't *add value* to your image, then it's likely *taking away* from your image. You want the props to be relevant, but you don't want them to draw attention *away* from your main subject. Keeping the scene uncluttered and simple is usually a good start because you want to showcase your main dish. Some examples of appropriate props and additions to your scene might include silverware, prepared food (such as side dishes or ingredients from the main dish), drink glasses, and napkins. Also, when photographing a finished, prepared meal, it's also best to avoid placing in your scene unprepared food items, such as whole peppers, potatoes, or onions. Instead, place food items that you would eat along with the meal or prepared items that can be added to the food (**Figure 3.20**). If it's something you wouldn't normally eat in its entirety (or in an uncooked state), then it's probably not going to seem very appetizing alongside your cooked food in a photograph.

Figure 3.20
I placed wafer cookies in the background of this image, which is something that I would likely want to eat with a sweet dessert and coffee.

Canon 5D Mark III · ISO 100 · 1.5 sec. · ƒ/5.6 · Canon 100mm ƒ/2.8L Macro lens

Figure 3.21
This is a selection of some of my dishes for food photography; many of them are handmade.

Canon 5D Mark III · ISO 100 · 1/4 sec. · ƒ/11 · Canon 24–70mm ƒ/2.8L lens

Figure 3.22
I love shopping at antique stores for unique and intricate utensils.

Canon 5D Mark III · ISO 1250 · 1/125 sec. · ƒ/6.7 ·
Canon 24–70mm ƒ/2.8L lens

Dishes and Accessories

When selecting the plates and utensils to use in your photograph, you want to match them to your food. However, the colors, dishes, and utensils you use will also reflect your own personal style. I used to use a lot of white dishes but since then have moved to metal, wood, and handmade ceramic items (**Figure 3.21**). I like to search through thrifts stores, antique shops, and estate sales to find unique dishes and utensils (**Figure 3.22**), and I even have a small ceramic studio where I make many of my own. My goal is to create and use dishes that complement the food I am photographing, but that are never too bright or overdone. I prefer simple, muted colors with a bit of texture. Overall, there's really no rule to what dishes you should use—just go with what you think fits your style and your food.

The size of the dish is also important. I collect a lot of smaller plates and bowls and use them often in my photographs. Putting food on a plate that is a little smaller than one you might normally use to eat on gives the appearance that there is more on the plate and that the food item is larger than it actually is (**Figure 3.23**). It also makes composing the photograph that much easier because it is difficult to frame a scene with a plate that is only half (or less) full. This also works well with silverware— I often use small salad forks and smaller spoons off to the side of my dishes to give the appearance that the food is bigger than it actually is.

Figure 3.23
**Using small bowls
is a great choice
for food photog-
raphy, especially
when you want to
accentuate the size
of small foods like
blueberries.**

Canon 5D Mark III ·
ISO 100 · 1/8 sec. ·
ƒ/8 · Canon 100mm
ƒ/2.8L Macro lens

There are a lot of great places you can find dishes, cups, and utensils for your photographs. I like to shop at stores where I can buy individual items, instead of having to buy an entire set (I typically use only one or two of the same dish in a scene). Thrift stores and yard sales are also good places to score unique dishes and accessories for really great prices. Another place I like to shop is craft stores. They often have interesting glassware and decorative items that are intended for other purposes (candles, for example) but that can be used as cups or bowls in photographs. I have also been known to purchase plates directly from restaurants, just like I did with this interesting metal plate I discovered at a local pizza restaurant (**Figure 3.24**).

Figure 3.24
I purchased this metal plate from a local pizza restaurant after admiring it during my meal.
Canon 5D Mark III · ISO 100 · 6 sec. · f/8 · Canon 100mm f/2.8L Macro len

Textiles and Textures

Adding texture to a photograph is a good way to lend a sense of depth and realism to the scene, and there are many ways to add texture with food photography. I do this by using textured tabletops and textiles, such as napkins and tablecloths (**Figure 3.25**). I have a large selection of fabric to choose from, and some of my favorites are scarves I purchased during my travels overseas. I also use common household items, such as cheese-cloth, for a nice textured and rustic look below some of my dishes (**Figure 3.26**).

I also like to add a small napkin to many of my scenes. If you pay careful attention to my photographs, you will likely see the same napkins used over and over again. Another secret of mine is that they are not even napkins at all! In fact, they are hankies that I found at a thrift store several years back. Their size makes them perfect as an accessory in my photographs, and the few that I use are generic enough that I can reuse them in more than one photograph.

Figure 3.25
This is just a small sample of many of the fabrics I use with my food photography. As you can see, I am very fond of the color blue!

Canon 5D Mark III • ISO 1250 • 1/125 sec. • f/6.7 • Canon 24–70mm f/2.8L lens

Figure 3.26
Cheesecloth is an excellent textile to use with food photography; it is a great way to add texture while still being a subtle element in the scene.

Canon 5D Mark III ·
ISO 100 · 6 sec. ·
ƒ/5.6 · Canon 100mm
ƒ/2.8L Macro lens

Textured wood tabletops are also a nice addition to any food photographer's prop stash. If you want to use a textured tabletop, they are pretty easy to make on your own. You just need a thin piece of wood big enough to cover the table, a few different colors of paint, and you can even "crackle" the surface with special paint (you can usually find all of this at hardware or craft stores). You can also scour yard sales and antique stores for old wooden doors or just use any other type of old wood that you can find lying around the house. In the past, I have used wood from an old fence, and I even purchased some weathered barn wood from an online retailer, both which made for some nice surfaces.

Right now, my table of choice is a special table made specifically for my food photography (**Figure 3.27**). It's a set of two nesting tables—one for eye-level photographs, and the other for overhead work—with several interchangeable tabletops, including weathered wood, faux concrete, and even rusted metal. It's perfect for the work I do and makes it easy to change up the look of a photograph just by changing out the tabletop.

If you are short on space, or just don't want to deal with full-sized tabletops, then vinyl tabletop backdrops might be a good choice. These are large vinyl prints with wood, metal, or any photograph of a surface printed directly onto the vinyl. You can purchase

Figure 3.27
This food photography table, custom-designed and built by Kula Solutions in Portland, Oregon, consists of two nesting tables and five reversible interchanging tabletops.
Canon 5D Mark III ·
ISO 100 ·
HDR Exposure ·
Canon 24–70mm
ƒ/2.8L lens

them online, or you can find a print shop that prints onto vinyl and make your own. One downside to using vinyl backdrops is that they have a protective layer added to them, which can add a texture to the vinyl that may make the surface look less realistic, especially when photographing food up-close. They also tend to reflect light much more than you would see with natural materials, which can make the surface look less like wood (**Figure 3.28**). There are other similar materials you can use, so it's best to do your research and find something that works well for you.

Figure 3.28
This food was photographed on a vinyl backdrop using backlight. Note the glare coming from the tabletop that would not be present with a standard wood surface.

Fuji X-T1 • ISO 200 • 0.5 sec. • ƒ/5.6 • Fuji XF 18–135mm ƒ/3.5-5.6R LM OIS WR lens

Chapter 3 Challenges

There are a lot of different ways you can add to the look of your food photographs through styling and adding props, so here are a few challenges to get you started.

Make It Messy

Cook up a meal and set it up to photograph. Make the food itself and area around it as clean as possible, and take a few photos. Then, add some crumbs, make some drips, or drop a few bits around the plate (berries, seeds, nuts, and so on). Take a few photos of this setup. Compare the two images to see whether one gives a different, more realistic feel over the other.

Play with Props

Create a dish that requires the use of a utensil, such as a spoon or fork. Go through several different styles and sizes of utensils and place them in your scene, one at a time, photographing the setup after each replacement. Take a look at your photos. Do any look better than others? Which styles and sizes of utensil were most effective?

Bulk It Up

Cook a bowl of soup with noodles, such as chicken noodle soup or Japanese Udon noodles, and then set aside two bowls—one with nothing in it and one with some clear glass stones placed halfway up the bowl. Pour portions into both of the bowls, and notice how the noodles look in each.

Share your results with the book's Flickr group! Join the group here: flickr.com/groups/ foodphotographyfromsnapshotstogreatshots

Canon 5D Mark III •
ISO 100 • 0.5 sec. •
ƒ/5.6 • Canon 100mm
ƒ/2.8L Macro lens

4

Framing and Composition

Improve Your Photos with Strong Compositional Elements

To make a beautiful food photograph, you need more than just knowledge about your camera and what settings to use. You should also have a good understanding of how to compose your images. In fact, I consider composition to be one of the most challenging aspects of photography. Being able to create beautiful compositions is an extremely useful skill and is sometimes more important than the nitty-gritty technical aspects of photography. Just knowing one or two tricks isn't enough, but learning several methods and piecing them together will help you to create great food photographs. In this chapter, you will examine how you can add interest to your photos by using common compositional elements.

Poring Over the Picture

Every so often, it's nice to have something sweet. I don't consider myself much of a baker, but I had some leftover berries, a good pie crust recipe, and company coming over, so I decided that I would make a simple galette, which is basically a flattened-out pie. Because it was flat and didn't have much height to it, I photographed it from an overhead view to highlight its shape.

Placing additional berries in the scene added color and substance.

Canon 5D Mark III • ISO 100 • 4 sec. • ƒ/4.5 • Canon 24–70mm ƒ/2.8L II lens

I positioned the galette in the right third of the frame for a balanced composition.

I sprinkled powdered sugar on and around the pastry to make the scene look messy and realistic.

I chose an intricate spoon to add some flair to the image.

Cherry blossoms carefully scattered throughout the scene add substance to the photograph.

Canon 5D Mark III • ISO 100 • 1/10 sec. • f/5.6 • Canon 100mm f/2.8L Macro lens

I used an aperture wide enough to blur the background yet still keep the details visible in the scene.

When Spring finally arrived in Portland, I wanted to find a way to integrate it with my food photography. So, I came up with a simple setup where I could add cherry blossoms as a garnish. This small ramekin filled with yogurt and jam was the perfect scene with which to use the delicate pink flowers.

Finding Balance

There are really no solid rules when it comes to photography as a whole, but there are standard techniques you can apply to a photograph to make it more attractive. When I photograph food, I am always trying to find balance—whether with the placement of items within the frame, the angle of my lens, the distance I photograph from, or other elements. Here are a few basic guidelines that will help you find balance for many food photographs.

Figure 4.1
I positioned the spoon so that the main portion of the scoop was in the upper-right third of the image.

Canon 5D Mark II • ISO 100 • 0.3 sec. • f/8 • Canon 72–200mm f/4L IS lens

The Rule of Thirds

One way to balance an image is to position a main focal point on a "third-line" in the frame. The *Rule of Thirds* is a basic composition principle that exists in all forms of visual art, and using it can often result in a pleasing, well-balanced image. To understand, picture a tic-tac-toe grid placed over your image, and notice how it divides the image into thirds vertically and horizontally. "Proper" placement of your subject would be along any of the grid lines or at any of the four intersecting points within the frame (**Figure 4.1**).

Now, this doesn't mean that putting the food in the middle of the frame won't look good (**Figure 4.2**). Symmetry—as well as asymmetry—can also be beautiful. There is no right or wrong way to compose a photograph, but there are always ways that will make a specific subject or setup look better. Because all photos are unique, it's a good idea to experiment with your subject to see what type of framing works best.

Figure 4.2
A center-positioned framing was perfect for this bowl of noodles.
....
Canon 5D Mark II · ISO 100 · 1/8 sec. · ƒ/8 · Canon 72–200mm ƒ/4L IS lens

Background and Foreground

When composing your food photographs, don't forget to pay careful attention to the background and foreground elements. Items that are not featured or in focus within the photograph can still have a significant impact, so it's important that you are aware of them. Not only do you want these items to look good, you also want to make sure that their placement is appropriate and pleasing.

You'll want to be especially careful of where these background and foreground elements exit the frame. I will often move things around so that they are positioned in the corners of the image (**Figures 4.3**). I find that this gives balance to the main subject without drawing too much attention to the background.

Another thing to keep in mind when placing the items in your scene is to be aware of how they are "touching" each other in the photograph. For many of my images, I intentionally keep certain elements from intersecting and touching in the frame whenever possible (**Figure 4.4**). This is a good way to add a balanced flow in the photo. It's not a steadfast rule, but it's something to at least try your hand at when photographing food to see whether it helps with the overall composition.

Figure 4.3
When positioning items in the background, I often place them in the corners of the frame.

Figure 4.4
I am usually careful to keep items from "touching" the main subject in my photographs. Notice how the fig in the foreground has room around it and that it is not overlapping any of the other figs in the background.

Canon 5D Mark III • ISO 100 • 3 sec. • ƒ/5.6 • Canon 100mm ƒ/2.8L Macro lens

Canon 5D Mark III • ISO 100 • 1/8 sec. • ƒ/6.7 • Canon 100mm ƒ/2.8L Macro lens

Triangles and Groups of Threes

Finding or creating triangles in a scene is another simple way to add balance to a food photograph. This doesn't mean you are actually adding triangle-shaped items to your image but rather that you are placing elements within the frame so that they form a triangle shape when you "connect the dots" (**Figure 4.5**). The reason that triangles are pleasing in an image, regardless of how subtle they are, is that they keep the viewer's

Figure 4.5
This group of ramekins forms a triangle shape when you connect the dots. This helps keep the viewer's eyes on the image.

Canon 5D Mark III • ISO 100 • 0.3 sec. • ƒ/5.6 •
Canon 100mm ƒ/2.8L Macro lens

Figure 4.6
I often add elements to my scene in groups of three. In this example, I placed three raspberries in the foreground to balance out the shot.

Canon 5D Mark III • ISO 100 • 1/15 sec. • ƒ/5.6 •
Canon 100mm ƒ/2.8L Macro lens

eyes on the photo. By following a triangle with his or her eyes, the viewer is basically circling around the image, looking at all the elements.

Another simple way to add balance to your photos is to think in groups of three. This is easy to do when styling your food, not only with the number of objects you are photographing, such as muffins or pieces of fruit, but also with garnishes. You can even deliberately place small items, crumbs, or drips on a plate in groups of three to create subtle triangle shapes in your photograph (**Figure 4.6**).

Perspective and Framing

Sometimes a well-lit scene and beautifully styled dish just aren't enough. Finding the best position from which to photograph your food can make a big impact on the look and feel of the image.

Vertical and Horizontal

There are two ways you can frame your photograph: vertically or horizontally. Most types of foods photograph well both ways, especially if you're photographing something on a plate or in a bowl (**Figures 4.7** and **4.8**). I experiment with different framing positions for my images and usually end up finding several ways to photograph one setup.

Figure 4.7
My original framing for this setup was to photograph it in a vertical orientation.

Canon 5D Mark III •
ISO 100 • 1/20 sec. •
f/4 • Canon 100mm
f/2.8L Macro lens

Figure 4.8
The setup also works well as a horizontal image.

Canon 5D Mark III • ISO 100 • 1/10 sec. • f/5.6 •
Canon 100mm f/2.8L Macro lens

As a general rule, if I'm photographing something tall, I will frame it vertically (**Figure 4.9**). If I'm photographing something wide and want to capture the entire object, I'll photograph it horizontally (**Figure 4.10**). Yet there may be times when you need to break the rules (perhaps when photographing for a cookbook or magazine) and frame your food a specific way. This is when you'll have to get creative with your perspective, positioning, and maybe even styling to ensure a working setup for the framing of the final output.

Figure 4.9
It usually works best to photograph tall items vertically, like this shot of a blender filled with fruit.

Canon 5D Mark II ·
ISO 100 · 1/8 sec. ·
ƒ/8 · Canon 70–200mm
ƒ/4L IS lens

Figure 4.10
To photograph the entire plate of food, I decided a horizontal composition was the best choice.

Canon 5D Mark II • ISO 100 • 1/10 sec. • f/8 • Canon 70–200mm f/4L IS lens

Three-Quarters

The three-quarters angle is a pleasing one for food. It's similar to looking down at food from the same angle you would if you were about to eat it, which is probably why I use this perspective a lot. I find that it showcases the food well. Using a three-quarters angle is especially necessary with food inside a bowl, or for any kind of dish that has depth, because you want to be sure that the food is visible. By partially looking down on the dish, you can see it clearly (**Figure 4.11**).

Figure 4.11
When photographing something inside of a bowl, a three-quarters angle is usually the best choice.

Canon 5D Mark III • ISO 160 • 1/125 sec. • ƒ/5.6 • Canon 100mm ƒ/2.8L Macro lens

Eye Level

Another technique you can use is to position yourself at eye level to the table (**Figure 4.12**). This angle can help make the food you are photographing look taller and larger and is also good angle to use when photographing drinks.

Figure 4.12
Photographing this small plate of French toast with blueberries at eye level helped make the food appear much larger than it actually was.

Canon 5D Mark III •
ISO 100 • 1 sec. •
ƒ/8 • Canon 100mm
ƒ/2.8L Macro lens

Overhead View

Using an overhead view, or photographing straight down on your subject, is a good angle if you want to show a lot of things at once from a unique perspective (**Figures 4.13** and **4.14**). One of the reasons I enjoy this perspective is because it can help create a graphical image with a strong composition. This angle tends to work better with items that are short because having very little distance between the tops of your food and the other items means you're more likely to have everything in focus, even at a wide aperture.

Figure 4.13
An overhead view is a good choice for food that is flat, like this berry-filled galette.

Canon 5D Mark III •
ISO 100 • 4 sec. •
ƒ/4.5 • Canon 24–70mm
ƒ/2.8L II lens

Figure 4.14
Photographing from overhead can add an artistic and graphical element to your food, like this shot of shrimp I photographed at a market in Thailand.

Fuji X-T1 • ISO 1600 •
1/125 sec. • ƒ/5 •
Fuji XF 18–55mm
ƒ /2.8–4 R LM OIS lens

Focal Length, Lens Compression, and Depth of Field

The choices you make regarding gear, settings, and so on, have a great impact on the composition of an image. One of these choices is focal length because the lenses you choose affect the look of the background elements in your photographs. Keep on reading to learn how you can alter the composition and compress the background of an image just by changing your focal length.

What Is Lens Compression?

Lens compression is a way of distorting an image so that objects that are located behind or in front of the main focal point appear to be closer and larger than they really are. But don't let the word *distorting* scare you away. It doesn't distort the actual subject you're photographing like a wide-angle lens would, but rather it affects the background and foreground of your images by making them appear closer to the main subject. Adding compression to food photographs is something I do all the time, and it's actually one of my favorite techniques in photography.

Why Focal Length Matters

The focal length of your lens makes a big difference in the amount of lens compression you will see in a photograph. Basically, the longer the lens is, the more compression you can introduce.

As you can see in the overhead photo (**Figure 4.15**), I positioned the items in a line so that there is 1 foot between each one and the next, for a total distance of 2 feet between the apple and the orange. In **Figure 4.16**, I photographed the same setup at four focal lengths: 28mm, 50mm, 100mm, and 200mm. The aperture for each photograph is set to ƒ/16 so you can see the difference in the depth of field between the four focal lengths. The orange in the photo taken at 28mm is small compared to the orange in the photo taken at 200mm. You can also see how the foreground (the table) in the photo appears to get closer to the apple as the length of the lens increases.

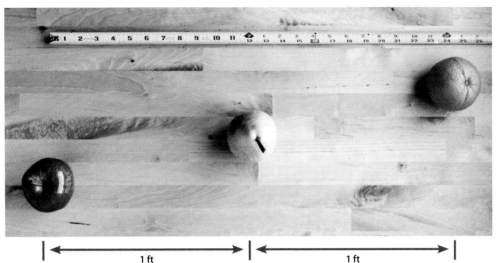

Figure 4.15
This is the setup for the Figure 4.16 series. There is a total of 2 feet between the apple and the orange. Each piece of fruit remained in this exact position for each of the following photos.

Canon 5D Mark II · ISO 100 · 1/40 sec · f/8 · 50mm lens

Canon 5D Mark II · ISO 100 · 0.4 sec · f/16 · 28mm lens

Canon 5D Mark II · ISO 100 · 0.4 sec · f/16 · 50mm lens

Figure 4.16
There is a total of 2 feet between the apple and the orange. Each piece of fruit remained in this exact position for each of the following photos. The aperture remained constant throughout each frame; the only thing that changed was the focal length and positioning of the camera.

Canon 5D Mark II · ISO 100 · 0.4 sec · f/16 · 70–200mm lens

Canon 5D Mark II · ISO 100 · 0.4 sec · f/16 · 70–200mm lens

Figure 4.17
These four images were all photographed at different apertures to show how the background of the image can change using different *f*-stops.

Canon 5D Mark III • ISO 100 • 1/6 sec. • *f*/2.8 • Canon 100mm *f*/2.8L Macro lens

Canon 5D Mark III • ISO 100 • 0.3 sec. • *f*/4 • Canon 100mm *f*/2.8L Macro lens

You can also use lens compression to add creative flair to a photograph. When you introduce compression to an image, you can significantly decrease the depth of field, giving you a softer bokeh and beautifully out-of-focus background. The easiest way to compress and blur the background in your images is to use a long focal length coupled with a somewhat wide aperture (**Figure 4.17**). You should place a good amount of distance between the camera and the subject, and between the subject and its background, if you want to decrease your depth of field as much as possible.

Focus

Focus is an important element in photography, yet with food photography it can be tricky to know exactly *where* to focus your lens. This is even more critical to grasp if you are using a wide aperture with a shallow depth of field, because much of the photograph will be out of focus, and the spot that is in focus will stand out even more. In this section, I discuss how to determine where to place your focus point, along with some tips and tricks for focusing your lens to get sharp, well-focused images.

f/5.6

f/11

Canon 5D Mark III · ISO 100 · 0.7 sec. · *f*/5.6 ·
Canon 100mm *f*/2.8L Macro lens

Canon 5D Mark III · ISO 100 · 3 sec. · *f*/11 ·
Canon 100mm *f*/2.8L Macro lens

Finding the Best Focus Point

It can be a challenge to decide where to put the focus point in your image. Often the best placement for focus is on one of the intersecting points of the Rule of Thirds, but this will vary from photo to photo. Some subjects will be trickier than others, so the best advice I can give is to try a few different placements and then take a look at the photos to see which focus point works best. Viewing the image on a computer, or even on your camera's LCD monitor, can help determine where the focus should be placed. Basically, if you're looking at your photo and your eyes are drawn to a certain point, that's probably where the focus should be.

Another general rule to follow is to focus on something in the photo that is close to you, as opposed to far away or in the middle of the dish. Even if there is a giant garnish on the top of a dish that really stands out, it might be the smaller garnish toward the front that your eyes are drawn to first (**Figure 4.18**). When I'm styling my food, I usually place a garnish deliberately as a specific point of focus and take a few photos with the focus on different areas around the dish just to make sure I have a nice, in-focus image that doesn't create too much tension for the viewer.

Figure 4.18

Although the simple solution for this image would be to focus on the green mint leaves, I chose to focus on the large sugar crystals on the top portion of the cake. This allowed more of the food to be in focus, and it also proved to be the place that my eye gravitates to when I look at the image.

Canon 5D Mark III · ISO 100 · 1/30 sec. · ƒ/8 · Canon 100mm ƒ/2.8L Macro lens

Focusing Tips and Tricks

When I'm using a tripod to photograph food, I always use the Live View feature on my camera (**Figure 4.19**). This not only allows me to compose the image well but also lets me zoom in to an area and focus on that specific spot. I also use manual focusing when on a tripod because it allows me the most control. If you are using a mirrorless camera with an electronic viewfinder, then you can preview what the final image will look like even before pressing the shutter. Overall, it's best to preview your images before moving on to ensure your focus is in the correct location.

Figure 4.19

I always use the Live View mode on my camera when photographing from a tripod. It not only gives me a clearer picture of what my image will look like but also allows me to zoom in and carefully manually focus my shot.

Fuji X-T1 • ISO 400 • 1/140 sec. • ƒ/2.2 • Zeiss Touit 32mm ƒ/1.8 lens

Shapes, Lines, and Colors

The shapes and colors of the elements in your photograph are just as important as the food itself. Being selective and aware of the types of dishes, napkins, garnishes, and tabletops you use, along with the framing of your scene, can help improve the overall look of your food photograph.

Shapes

Paying close attention to the shapes in your image can help with your composition. This is one reason that I prefer to use circular plates for most of my dishes (**Figure 4.20**). I like the way the plate curves near the corners of an image, and you can more easily frame and compose your photos when you don't have to avoid the harsh corners of square plates and bowls.

Lines and Corners

As I mentioned earlier in the chapter, placing elements in the corners of your images can help with the balance of the photograph. Watch for lines in your images, and be aware of where those lines point and lead. Lines may be created by the food, the silverware, the tabletop, or the background elements (**Figure 4.21**). It's a good idea to point these lines toward the corners of the dish.

Figure 4.20
I prefer to use circular plates for most of my food photography.

Canon 5D Mark III •
ISO 100 • 1/8 sec. •
ƒ/5.6 • Canon 100mm
ƒ/2.8L Macro lens

Figure 4.21
When adding flatware to a scene, I will often point it toward one of the corners of the image.

Canon 5D Mark III • ISO 100 • 1/6 sec. • ƒ/4.5 • Canon 100mm ƒ/2.8L Macro lens

Colors

When we look at a photograph, our eyes are attracted to the brightest parts of the image first, and then they navigate throughout the rest of the photo. When you're photographing food, you probably have a main subject that you want to highlight, so it's important to set up your photo so that your viewer's eyes go straight toward the food and are not overly distracted by anything else, such as a colored napkin or bright food placed in the background of the scene.

If you have a photograph in which the colors weigh heavily to one color group and it looks like it still "needs something," a good way to balance it out is to add a complementary color to the scene. A complementary color is one that sits opposite a given color on a standard color wheel (**Figure 4.22**). Using these opposite colors, even in small quantity, can liven up a photo and make it "pop" (**Figure 4.23**).

Figure 4.22
A color wheel is a useful tool when you want to add color to a photograph.

Figure 4.23
For this image of a fruit salad, I complemented the pink hue of the watermelon by using a turquoise-lined bowl, as well as a soft-green placemat.

Canon 5D Mark III • ISO 100 • 1/125 sec. • ƒ/5.6 • Canon 100mm ƒ/2.8L Macro lens

You don't have to stick to the exact opposite color on the color wheel—staying within a general color group is a good guideline. You also don't even need to follow this at all. Using a complementary color in your food image is usually best when the image looks unbalanced, with one dominant color.

Sometimes, however, you may want to exaggerate the colors of your dish by adding items of the same color around it. This could be done with silverware, tabletops, napkins, drinks, garnishes in the dish, and so on. In **Figure 4.24,** I chose to enhance the blue from the blueberries by using a blue placemat below the bowl. Oatmeal doesn't have much color on its own, and so intensifying the blues in the scene made the image much more appealing.

Figure 4.24
I used a blue place-mat to enhance the color of the blueberries.

Canon 5D Mark II •
ISO 100 • 1/6 sec. •
ƒ/8 • Canon 70–200mm
ƒ/4L IS lens

Chapter 4 Challenges

Once you have a basic understanding of why an image looks good, you can apply that to your own photographs. Using different angles, shapes, and colors in your food images can enhance an already tasty-looking dish. Here are a few challenges to help you get started.

Framing and Using Different Perspectives

Set up a plate of food and photograph it both vertically and horizontally, regardless of your subject. Move items in the background and foreground and position them on the table so that they look best for each setup. See which one you like best.

Next, photograph the same setup from three different perspectives: overhead, three-quarters, and eye level. Feel free to move the food or other items around to create balance. Watch how the background changes as you change your position and how each perspective changes the overall feel of the photograph.

Using Lens Compression

If you have lenses of varying focal lengths, try creating your own versions of the compression examples I showed in Figure 4.16. Find two or more different items, place them on a table, and photograph them with different lenses. (It's a good idea to use a tripod for this challenge.) Try to keep the front-most item the same size in the frame for each photo, which will require you to move your position forward or backward, depending on which lens you are using. Also, try keeping the aperture the same for each photograph so you can see how each focal length affects depth of field.

Playing with Color

Set up a dish with one dominant color, such as a bunch of berries in a white bowl. Then, select an item to place in the scene that is similar in color to the berries (such as another bowl, a utensil, or a place-mat). Photograph it and then swap out the item for a similar item in an opposite color from the berries on the color wheel. Preview the images. Which one do you prefer?

Share your results with the book's Flickr group! Join the group here: flickr.com/groups/ foodphotographyfromsnapshotstogreatshots

Fuji X-T1 · ISO 1000 ·
1/25 sec. · ƒ/1.8 ·
Zeiss 32mm ƒ/1.8 lens

5
Let's Get Social

Setting Yourself Up for Online Success

Sharing your food photographs on the Internet is an important part of making yourself known as a photographer, recipe creator, or cookbook author. And if you want to turn your passion for food and photography into a business, then you will need to make certain that your online presence is well established. In this chapter, I will discuss some tips, resources, and ideas to get your brain churning and help you find your way in the ever-growing industry of social media and networking.

Keep in mind that this is only the tip of the iceberg! There are entire books dedicated to the type of content I will be sharing in the next few pages. In fact, to help you out even further, I created a page on my own website with the links, services, and information I mention throughout this chapter, as well as some other information to help get you started. To view that content, please go to http://foodbook.nicolesy.com.

Poring Over the Picture

I used two of my own handmade ceramic dishes to give the scene a more rustic look.

I drenched the berries in syrup to make them shiny and more appetizing.

Canon 5D Mark III •
ISO 100 • 2 sec. •
f/9.5 • Canon 100mm
Macro f/2.8L lens

An overhead view shows off the different shapes and textures in the scene.

I left a small amount of empty space to the right to balance the composition.

Blueberries are one of my favorite fruits and garnishes to use in my food photographs. They have a lot of color and even have texture when positioned in certain ways. I originally photographed this dish at eye-level to show the height of the berries piled on top of the French toast. After taking a quick snapshot with my iPhone from overhead, however, I quickly realized how good it looked and re-photographed it with my DSLR from the same vantage point.

Poring Over the Picture

I photographed this from overhead to feature several items on the table at once.

I focused on the center bowl and made sure that the entire dish was in the frame.

Fuji X-T1 • ISO 200 •
1/100 sec. • ƒ/5.6 •
Fuji 18-55mm
ƒ/2.8–4 lens

The noodles to the right
add a sense of minimalism
and balance to the scene.

I enjoy using my food photography skills while I am traveling
abroad, just like I did with this overhead photograph of soup in
Chiang Mai, Thailand. The trick is to find food that is in good
light or seat yourself in the restaurant so that you have the
best light in the room (diffused window light is ideal). Another
required skill is speed! Try to take your photographs as quickly
as possible so that you can eat your food while it is still fresh.

Your Website Is Your Online Home

Whether it is a personal blog or a business website, having a place just for you and your work is an essential part of building your online brand and presence. Social media and photo-sharing sites are great (and I'll discuss those later in this chapter), but building an online space that you control is the best way to ensure that you have a place to share your content. It also gives other people, such as clients, friends, or fellow photographers, an easy way to find out how to contact you, as well as learn more about you and your work.

This section is all about you and your website. Maybe you already have a website set up where you share your photographs and other content, and if that's you, then you may already have a good grasp on what I will be sharing in this section. However, don't jump ahead too quickly! Digital content changes at a rapid pace, so you might learn about a few things that you had never considered. And for those of you who are ready to get started in creating your own website and portfolio, then keep on reading!

Setting Up a Website and Blog

If you are setting up a website for the first time, it might feel a little overwhelming, especially if you have little experience with web design, coding, and all of the minor details involved with the process. You could hire a designer to do the work for you, but those costs can really add up. If you would like to do it yourself, the good news is that many services make setting it up as simple (or as advanced) as you would like.

First, there are some free services you can look into. Two popular options, Wordpress.com and Blogger.com, enable you to build a good starting blog. However, these (and other free options) will eventually have their limits, such as you won't be able to customize them as much as you may prefer, so in time you may want to upgrade to something that is a little more robust.

I currently use Wordpress.*org* (not to be confused with Wordpress.*com*), which enables you to build a fully customized website but can also require certain coding and design skills at times, especially when setting it up (**Figure 5.1**). I'm not a professional web designer, but I know just enough to do it myself, so I was able to get my website up and running (and maintained) without having to hire help. (You can view my Wordpress.org website by going to http://nicolesy.com.)

Figure 5.1
This is a screenshot of what my Wordpress.org blog looked like while I was writing this book. I am able to customize every aspect of my website and find myself making design changes over time. If you go to my website, it might look different now than what you see here in this book (http://nicolesy.com).

Wordpress.org is free to download, but the extras add up. First, you will need to host the website on a server, so you will incur a monthly server fee with that. You will also need a custom domain (URL), which is another annual fee paid to a domain registrar. Then, you will need a theme (the template that determines the design of the site), and while you *can* use free themes, you will probably want to opt for one that is more able to suit your style. There is a lot you can do with Wordpress, but it does take some commitment to get it up and running on your own.

Another option for an easy-to-create professional website is Squarespace.com (**Figure 5.2**). This is probably the simplest to set up and requires no design or coding experience. The interface to get started and post a blog or portfolio is all WYSIWYG (which

> **Note**
>
> For links and resources for the items listed in this section, please visit http://foodbook.nicolesy.com.

stands for "what you see is what you get"), so it's easy to build it without things being overly complicated. Squarespace is an all-in-one service with a monthly fee, and it allows you to create a blog, portfolio, e-commerce store, and more. It's a good site to check out if you want a professional website but don't have the chops to do it yourself.

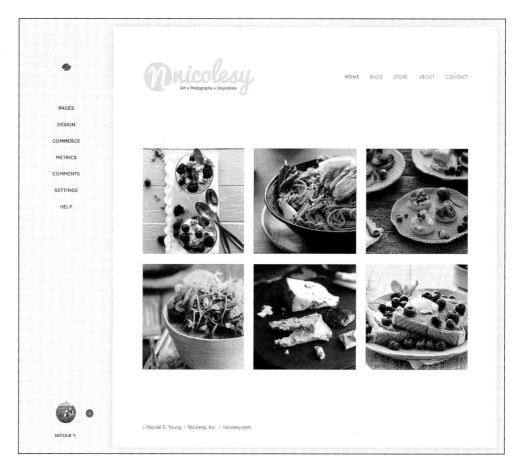

Figure 5.2
This is an example of the Squarespace interface.

Setting Up Your Portfolio

If you're a photographer, odds are that you will want to display your work somewhere online. A portfolio filled with your own food photographs is the best way to show potential clients and publishers the types of photographs you are capable of creating. It also gives insight to your skills and abilities.

You have many options when choosing a platform to build your portfolio. If you already have a website, then your theme or service may offer an option to include an integrated portfolio right alongside your blog. This is a great option because it keeps people on your site but may not be available if you opt for a free blog (such as Wordpress.com or Blogger, for example).

If you need a third-party portfolio site, the great news is that there are many choices. Some are free to use, and some come with a monthly fee. Photo-sharing sites, like Flickr, Foodgawker, and Tastespotting, are good ways to get your work out there and seen. For a portfolio, however, you might want to present your work in a more elegant and professional way. 500px is a site that offers both free and affordable paid plans, as well as a dedicated portfolio option to present your work beautifully (**Figure 5.3**). There are also many other sites you can use, such as SmugMug.com, the website I use for my online portfolio (**Figure 5.4**). For more examples and links to other portfolio websites, please visit the resources site for this book (http://foodbook.nicolesy.com).

Figure 5.3
500px is a great and inexpensive option to use for your online portfolio and is also a place where you can license and sell prints of your work.

Figure 5.4
My main portfolio website is hosted at SmugMug, a website where photographers can store, share, and also sell their work to clients.

Sharing and Networking

Sharing your work and making your presence known is a good way to build your brand and your business and can even help you grow as a photographer in general. There are many different paths to success as a photographer, and what you choose to do will depend on your goals and personal strategy. Some photographers will focus on the imagery, while others will include writing and recipes to go with their food photographs in order to build a following. In this section, I discuss the different ways of "getting social" with your online presence, as well as ways to network with other like-minded people to help build you and your brand.

Grow a Social Media Presence

In this day and age, having a solid presence on social media is important for photographers and food bloggers. Whether it's via Instagram, Twitter, or Facebook, people are constantly online and communicating with each other through posts, comments, and other interactions (**Figure 5.5**). If you're not already on social media, then it might be something to consider jumping into sooner rather than later.

There are a lot of social media sites currently out there, with new ones popping up all the time. Although it's tempting to be part of as many as possible, you don't want to spread yourself too thin. It's best to stick with the sites that cater to your brand, your photography, and also where your audience will likely be found. Maybe this means that you share to Facebook because your primary audience is your friends and family. Or perhaps you are into video and want to reach a potentially larger audience on YouTube and monetize your creations. It's best to focus on the social sites that suit your style most closely.

Figure 5.5
The three main social media sites that I use regularly are Twitter, Instagram, and Facebook.

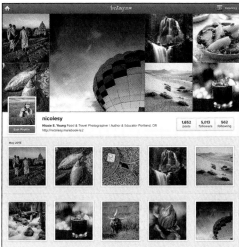

The tough part about social media is that your follower count, whether it's big or small, can be a double-edged sword. You may have few followers, so to outsiders your social media presence looks small. Those few followers, however, could, in fact, be loyal and engaging fans! On the flip side, you may have a *lot* of followers on one of your social media accounts yet the quality of those followers is subpar. I have seen both.

One thing I would caution against when it comes to social media sites is to not rely too heavily on them, and *definitely* don't use them as your only way of sharing content. Third-party websites and businesses have a habit of changing, sometimes in ways we don't always appreciate, and as a site fades in popularity (which they all will eventually) or the primary audience changes, so will your profile with that site. It's always a good idea to maintain your own website, blog, and portfolio where you hold 100 percent of the control.

Build a Mailing List

If there is one thing that I wish I had done *years* ago when I first created my website, it would have been to start collecting names for a newsletter mailing list. At the time, the thought of direct marketing to a select group of people was not even on my radar. Social media was in its early stages (Facebook had just debuted, and Twitter did not even exist), and my business was barely even started. My only focus was to improve my photography, and it did not occur to me how powerful it would be to build my own personal audience of subscribers.

To get started, first you need to create an account with a provider. Sure, you could do it all from your personal email, but websites that specialize in this type of product will give security, authentication, and also statistics and reports. There are several services you can use, and they typically will offer you to start out with a free account. The service I use is Mailchimp, which allows accounts to have a few thousand free subscribers before you have to pay anything. Other mailing list sites work similarly. And, as your list size increases, you will either pay per subscriber or pay per email that you send.

Signing up for an account is simple, but how do you get people to subscribe? There are different ways you can entice people to sign up. First, if you have a blog, you can add plug-ins and add-ons, such as a sign-up form in a sidebar or a pop-up that appears when visitors open the link. If people visit your site and like what they see, then they just might add their name to the list. Other ways of bringing in subscribers is to give something away for free, such as an e-book or recipe, for example. There are many ways to help grow your mailing list, and it is something that can take time. Just get creative, and have fun with it!

When taking advantage of direct email marketing, one of the biggest things to keep in mind is that you must follow the rules. There are some pretty strict regulations in place for direct marketing to help prevent and avoid spam, all which are regulated with the CAN-SPAM Act of 2003 (http://ftc.gov). It's a good idea to familiarize yourself with this information before you start sending out emails. Oftentimes, using services like Mailchimp will help keep you in line, but it is still good to know your limits.

How you use your newsletter will depend on what your goals are. I use mine to promote free articles on my website, as well as any upcoming products or books I have that have just been released (**Figure 5.6**). And it's possible that having a mailing list is not even something that is necessary for you to achieve your goals. It's just one of the many tools that you can use in your arsenal to grow your business as a food photographer.

Figure 5.6
This is an example of a typical newsletter I will send to my email subscribers.

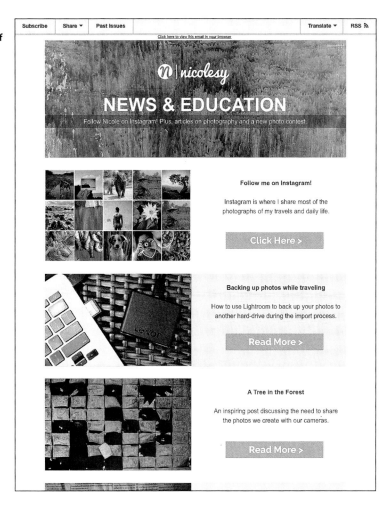

Attend Conferences

One of the best ways to create relationships and network with other individuals is through in-person conferences and get-togethers (**Figure 5.7**). Whether it is a food, blogging, or photography conference, you are guaranteed to find like-minded souls and probably have fun along the way. At these events, you can take classes to improve your skills, network with other bloggers and photographers, and possibly get face time with potential clients or publishers. It's also a great place to learn about trends and products coming onto the market.

There are a ton of conferences for both food bloggers and photographers out there, and I have listed some of them on my website for you to check out (http://foodbook.nicolesy.com).

Figure 5.7
Food blogging and photography conferences are a great way to meet other people with the same interests. Plus, the food is delicious, like this sushi that was served at an event during the 2014 International Food Blogger's Conference in Seattle, Washington.

Fuji X-T1 · ISO 1000 · 1/25 sec. · ƒ/1.8 · Zeiss 32mm ƒ/1.8 lens

Protecting Your Digital Content

Whether it's a blog post, photograph, or recipe that you created and shared online, odds are that you want to protect and control your digital content and intellectual property. There's nothing like a having popular website or brand share one of your photographs or recipes without your permission, especially when they fail to give credit to you, the original author.

Note

Please keep in mind that I am not an attorney. Any information shared in this chapter is to help you get started on safeguarding your intellectual property and should not be interpreted as sound legal advice. I highly encourage you to seek out a copyright lawyer for any legal counsel you may need regarding your business.

Register Your Copyright

If you are creating digital content and sharing it publicly online, the first step in protecting your content is to register the copyright for your photographs, recipes, and other items (such as books, e-books, and so on). Although your content is *technically* copyrighted by you from the moment of its creation, for that to hold up in court or in any type of legal battle (especially if you are seeking monetary damage), then you *must* have your copyright registered with the U.S. Copyright Office.

Registering your copyright is simpler than you think. You go to the website for the U.S. Copyright Office (http://copyright.gov) and follow the steps to registering your copyright. Because the process and steps can change over time, I won't go into detail here. Instead, to learn more about how to register your images, please go to the resources page on my own website (http://foodbook.nicolesy.com).

One thing to keep in mind with registering your work is that you will need to separate your published images versus your unpublished images. The U.S. Copyright Office considers something to be published once it is available for public display, distribution, or sale. So, if

Note

Please visit http://foodbook.nicolesy.com for links and resources on copyrighting your content.

you are posting content publicly to your website, that would be considered published content. You cannot mix published and unpublished works in one copyright registration claim, so it's a good idea to keep a folder of images set aside where you keep your published images.

I do my best to copyright a batch of my published photographs every quarter. I'll be honest, sometimes it is easier said than done (the government doesn't always make things easy), but it is good practice if you want to ensure that your content is protected.

Adding Copyright to Image Metadata

One thing you don't want to forget is to include the proper copyright information in the metadata of your photographs! This will help someone find the copyright owner (you!) if there is no other watermark or other information present on the image. You can oftentimes do this from in your camera (**Figure 5.8**) or by using a photo application such as Adobe Lightroom (**Figure 5.9**).

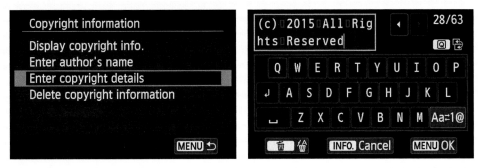

Figure 5.8
You can use your camera's settings to add your author name and copyright information, just like I did here with my Canon 70D.

Figure 5.9
Copyright information can be added to your images either using the Metadata panel in Lightroom's Library module or through a metadata preset, as shown here.

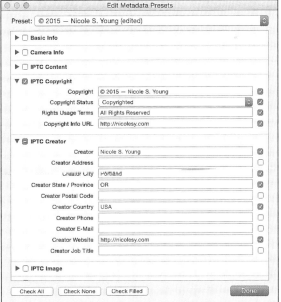

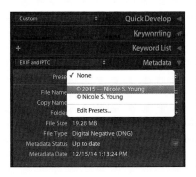

Use Watermarks on Images

Another simple way to help protect your content is through watermarks. Granted, they are not always foolproof, but they can sometimes prevent dishonest folks from lifting and reusing your images without your permission or knowledge.

Visible Watermarks

The first method of adding a watermark is to use an image or text overlay on your photo. Adding one is simple—you can use Photoshop, Lightroom, or even a dedicated application to apply them to your photos. This is the simplest form of protection, but depending on the overtness of the watermark, it can usually be easily cropped out.

So, what makes a good watermark? If you have a logo, that is usually a good option (**Figure 5.10**). Keep in mind that the main reason you are adding a watermark is either to prevent people from using the image or to bring people back to your website if they do. Not everyone, however, will be familiar with your logo. Using text is a good option as well because it allows you be very clear about your name and website (**Figure 5.11**). Or, if you like, try a combination of the two to make your brand and website very apparent (**Figure 5.12**).

Figure 5.10
Using a logo as your watermark is a good way to promote your brand.

Canon 5D Mark III ·
ISO 100 · 1.5 sec. ·
ƒ/5.6 · Canon 100mm
Macro ƒ/2.8L lens

Figure 5.11
Text, such as your name and website, are good ways to make it clear who owns the copyright and where to find you (the photographer).
Canon 5D Mark III • ISO 100 • 1.5 sec. • ƒ/5.6 • Canon 100mm Macro ƒ/2.8L lens

Figure 5.12
You can use a combination of both logo and text as a visible watermark on your photographs.
Canon 5D Mark III • ISO 100 • 1.5 sec. • ƒ/5.6 • Canon 100mm Macro ƒ/2.8L lens

I classify watermarks into two different categories: tacky and classy (**Figures 5.13** and **5.14**). A "tacky" watermark is a logo or text that is so intrusive on the photo that it is the main focus of the image. In other words, if you look at an image with a watermark and the watermark is the first (or only) thing you can see, then it's too much. However, this method is a good way to prevent almost anyone from using your photo, especially someone who is trying to get away with it. A classy watermark, on the other hand, is small, discreet, usually in a corner, and possibly even a little transparent. In other words, it blends well into the image. The downside to these is that they can be easily cropped or cloned out. However, if you have time to spare and want to get creative, then you could always try integrating the watermark into your image so that it is almost hidden but still very legible (**Figure 5.15**).

Figure 5.13
When a watermark is placed in the center of the photo, sometimes it is the only thing you see and is intrusive to the overall quality of the photograph.
Canon 5D Mark III • ISO 100 • 1 sec. • ƒ/8 • Canon 100mm Macro ƒ/2.8L lens

Figure 5.14
It's best to position a watermark in a location that will not interfere with the photograph.

Canon 5D Mark III •
ISO 100 • 1 sec. •
ƒ/8 • Canon 100mm
Macro ƒ/2.8L lens

Figure 5.15
You can also get creative with your watermark positioning and put it somewhere that is not noticeable until you look for it.

Canon 5D Mark III •
ISO 100 • 1 sec. •
ƒ/8 • Canon 100mm
Macro ƒ/2.8L lens

Digital Watermarks

If you prefer to not have a visible watermark on your image, then you may want to consider using a digital watermark. I prefer this method of watermarking and currently a plug-in called Digimarc® Guardian for Images because it allows me to share my images without a logo or text on the photograph (**Figure 5.16**). This plug-in requires either Adobe Photoshop or Photoshop Elements to work properly, and it also requires a paid subscription for Digimarc's services.

Figure 5.16
Believe it or not, this photograph is watermarked! I used Digimarc, which hides a digital watermark in the photo that is not always visible to the naked eye.

Canon 5D Mark III · ISO 100 · 1/30 sec · ƒ/5.6 · Canon 100mm Macro ƒ/2.8L lens

Once you sign up, install the plug-in (if necessary), and register your copy, adding a watermark is easy. Here's how it works:

1. First, prepare the image as you would any photograph to post online. I typically will use Lightroom to process my food photographs and then export as a web-sized JPEG image.

2. Next, open the image in Photoshop and go to Filters > Digimarc > Embed watermark.

3. Enter the copyright year and check other information as applicable. Select your level of watermarking (the higher the number, the more potential for the digital watermark to show in your photo) and then click OK.

4. There is now an invisible watermark embedded into the photo.

Another added benefit of Digimarc is that you can use its website to locate your photos; it will even auto-discover them for you (**Figure 5.17**). This makes it easy for you to create reports and locate where your digitally watermarked images are being used.

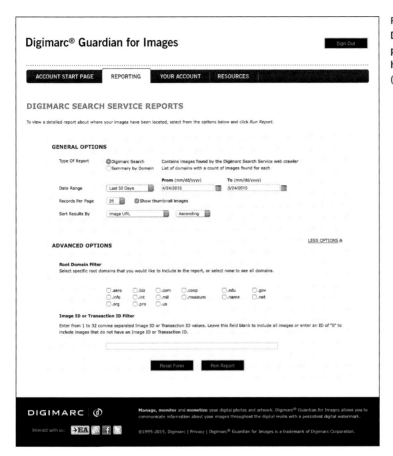

Figure 5.17
Digimarc allows you to run reports to locate photos with your digital watermark that have been found online posted. (http://www.digimarc.com/)

Protect Your Blog

If you have a website where you write articles or create recipes, you may also want to consider protecting the written content contained on that website. Keep in mind that the service you use to host your blog will determine the type of protection you can use on your website. I use Wordpress.org to create my blog, and because that is the software I am most familiar with, I will be using that as the basis for this section. However, I encourage you to do your own research to see what options you have with your platform of choice.

RSS Feed Protection

If you have a blog, then it likely also has an RSS feed. RSS stands for "Rich Site Summary" (and is also referred to as "Really Simple Syndication") and is a way to view articles and content from many different websites using a website or application (Feedly is one of the more popular options). The way it works is people subscribe to your blog; then every time you publish a post, subscribers will see it in their feeds. It's a great way to follow a certain set of blogs, but it is *also* a way for people to *repost your content* on their websites with your feed (also called *scraping*). Obviously, this is something you will want to prevent.

There are a few ways you can protect your content. First, you can allow only excerpts of your content to show up in the feed, such as one or two paragraphs, and then the user would need to visit your website to read the entire post. This seems ideal and it may work for some, but ultimately it could also prevent people from reading your entire post altogether if they don't click through. My personal preference is to read the full article inside the feed, and when I discover blogs that post only an excerpt in their RSS, then I will usually unsubscribe from them.

Another option (and my personal favorite) is to add a copyright footer to the bottom of each article (**Figure 5.18**). This will show up in the RSS feed only, and if someone is scraping your content, then they will look pretty silly when your copyright and website URL pop up at the bottom of each article. It's also a good way to remind your subscribers where the content is coming from.

Figure 5.18
One way to protect your blog posts is to add a footer to your RSS feeds, which will automatically apply to any of your future posts. You can see the information here on Feedly.com, an RSS aggregator, that I include on my articles when they are published.

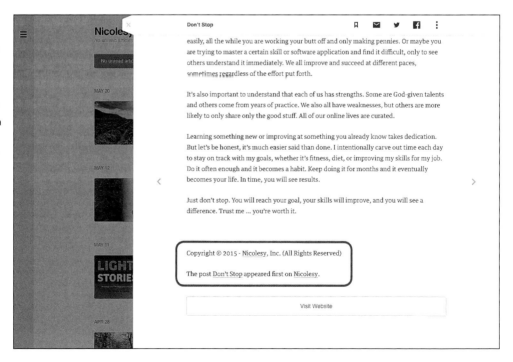

Right-Click and Copy Protection

If you are concerned with your text (as well as your images) being copied and pasted somewhere else, then one option you have is to add right-click and copy protection (**Figure 5.19**). This prevents users from right-clicking a photo to save it to their computer, as well as from highlighting and copying and pasting your words right off the page. There are also other ways to prevent certain types of sharing, such as pinning to Pinterest, for example.

These photos are copyrighted by their respective owners. All rights reserved. Unauthorized use prohibited.

Figure 5.19
Depending on the website service you use, you may be able to add right-click protection to your photos or the written content of your blog. Here I have right-click protection activated on the images in my Smug-Mug portfolio.

Do keep in mind that the more you secure your content to prevent it from being stolen, the more likely it is that your content will not be shared organically (or even shared at all). I would consider these options only as a last-resort or only for specific uses.

Note

For links and more information on these plug-ins, please visit http://foodbook.nicolesy.com.

Words of Wisdom

How you protect your content is ultimately up to you. For some, using a watermark is the best way to keep people from lifting your images, and some will also choose to keep their written content tightened down on their own websites. One important thing to keep in mind is that by *over-protecting* your content, however, you may also be preventing *honest people* from sharing it and bringing traffic to your website.

I can't tell you what to do with your intellectual property, but I can tell you what I do. First, I don't personally like visible watermarks on photographs. I used to add them, and still do on rare occasions, but when I post images on my blog or social media, I prefer to use a digital watermark so that it is hidden.

In terms of my blog, I use a plug-in that adds a footer to the RSS feed of each post, which links back to my website and also lists my business name as the copyright owner. I also make sure that any photo I post online is sized so that it is too small to print large but is also a good size so that viewers can see it full-size and see every detail.

Another thing I avoid is trying to contact every single small player who uses my images without my permission. A teenager who posts one of my images to his or her Tumblr page is really nothing to sweat over. Is what they did legal? Of course not. But it's important that I pick my battles and don't waste my time with each tiny inappropriate use.

The bottom line, for me, is choosing how to prevent the things that will hurt me in the long run if my property is stolen or used illegally. For example, I make most of my living through selling e-books in my online store. If someone were to try to resell one of my eBooks without my permission, then they would definitely be on thin ice with me (and my lawyer). Because I derive a large portion of my income through selling e-books and because I diligently register the copyright of my publications, the law would be on my side. For you, your main concern could be your photographs or the articles on your website. Protect your content how you see fit, and also choose your battles, in order find a way to make it all easily balance.

In the online world, it's almost impossible to prevent illegal use of your content. In fact, there are certain brands (such as recipe-sharing pages on Facebook, for example) whose entire collections of posts are derived through stealing other people's content. If you are a food blogger, you have probably either come across this at some point or have seen it happen to other colleagues. Overall it can be easy to get worked up over someone using your image and not giving you payment or credit, and sometimes there are easy ways to resolve these issues (such as flagging the content or contacting them directly to remove it). My advice is to not sweat the small stuff. If it is *not* a small use (such as a major company using your content without your permission) and if you have your legal ducks in a row, then the outcome might end up in your favor.

Chapter 5 Challenge

This chapter is all about information, and I hope you learned a thing or two! I don't have a lot of homework for you to do, so instead, I'll send you to my website for more information.

Visit the Resources Page

If you would like to find out more information about the items discussed in this chapter, then I have created an entire page on my website just for you! Here are some of the things you will find when you visit http://foodbook.nicolesy.com:

- Links to the websites and services mentioned in this chapter, along with some additional sites I felt were worth mentioning (but didn't have room to sneak into the book!)

- Tutorials and downloads on some of the content discussed in this chapter

- Articles and tutorials on food photography and styling

- Links to inspirational content and food blogs for you to get some creative ideas and become excited about your food photography

Canon 70D · ISO 100 ·
0.4 sec. · *f*/4 ·
Canon 50mm Macro lens

6

Processing Images with Adobe Lightroom

Making Your Photographs Look Their Best

As digital photographers, we cannot avoid processing, or editing, our photos. The good thing is that when editing food photographs, you usually won't use a lot of flair or crazy, off-the-wall editing techniques. My philosophy is to keep my photographs clean and make them look like they were not edited. Ironically, extensive editing can sometimes make a photo look as if it hasn't been edited, so I prefer to use simple, basic techniques that I apply subtly.

Although I included as much information in this chapter as I could about working in Adobe Lightroom, it is not an all-encompassing lesson on using the software. It does, however, cover many of the basics specific to organizing and editing your photographs. There is no right way to process any given image, but by using the techniques in this chapter, you will be off to a good start in developing your own style and overall editing workflow.

Poring Over Adobe Lightroom

The Library Module Workspace

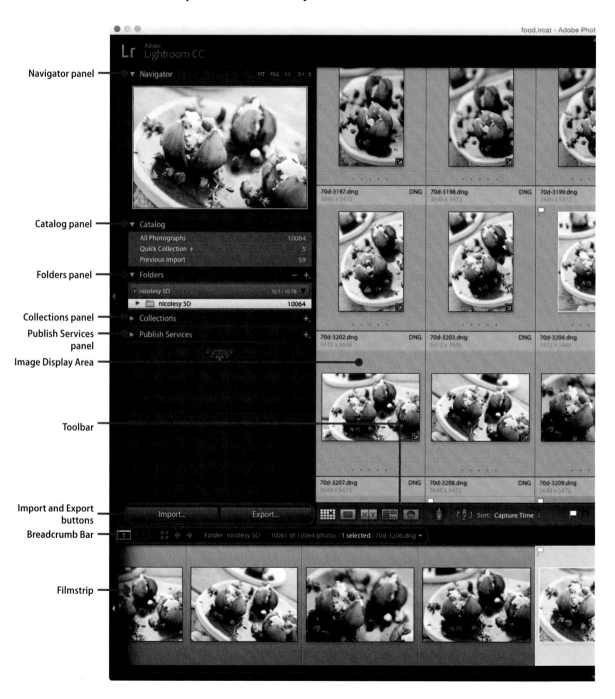

Navigator panel

Catalog panel

Folders panel

Collections panel

Publish Services panel

Image Display Area

Toolbar

Import and Export buttons

Breadcrumb Bar

Filmstrip

Module Picker

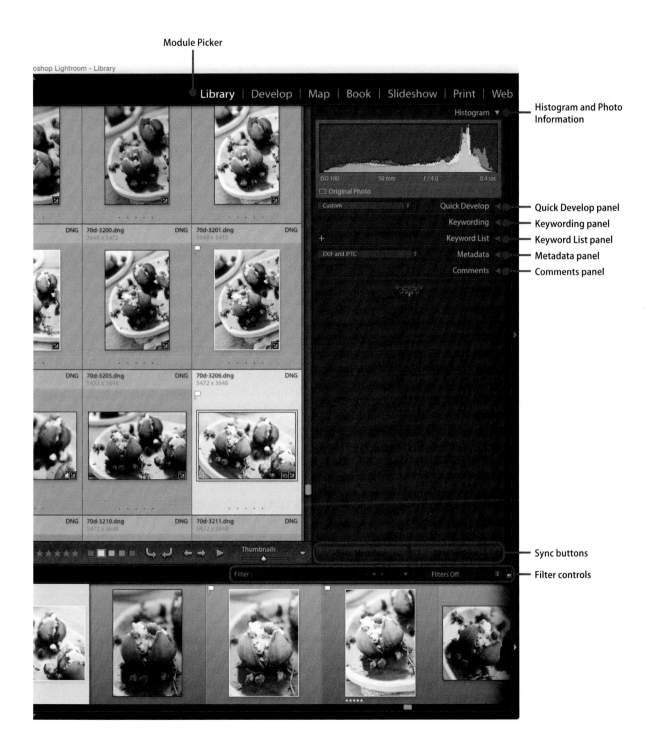

oshop Lightroom - Library

Library | Develop | Map | Book | Slideshow | Print | Web

Histogram ▼ — Histogram and Photo Information

ISO 100   50 mm   f / 4.0   0.4 sec

☐ Original Photo

Custom — Quick Develop — Quick Develop panel

Keywording — Keywording panel

\+ — Keyword List — Keyword List panel

EXIF and IPTC — Metadata — Metadata panel

Comments — Comments panel

DNG   70d-3200.dng   DNG   70d-3201.dng   DNG
3648 x 5472   3648 x 5472

DNG   70d-3205.dng   DNG   70d-3206.dng   DNG
5472 x 3648   5472 x 3648

DNG   70d-3210.dng   DNG   70d-3211.dng   DNG
5472 x 3648   5472 x 3648

★★★★★ ■□■■■ Thumbnails — Sync buttons

Filter :   Filters Off — Filter controls

The Develop Module Workspace

Navigator panel

Presets panel
Snapshots panel
History panel
Collections panel

Image Display Area

Toolbar

Copy and Paste buttons
Breadcrumb Bar

Filmstrip

Module Picker

Histogram and Photo Information

Tool Strip

Basic panel

Tone Curve panel

HSL/Color/B&W panel

Split Toning panel

Detail panel

Lens Correction panel

Effects panel

Camera Calibration panel

Previous and Reset buttons

Filter controls

Getting Started

Before you jump in to editing your photos, you'll want to understand a couple of things to make the editing process easier: monitor calibration and photo-editing software.

Calibrating Your Monitor

If you plan to share your photos on the Internet or through any type of computer interface, a color-calibrated monitor is essential to ensuring proper colors in your images. When you calibrate your monitor, you are setting up your screen so that it looks as balanced as possible. So if you edit a photo on your computer and post it on the Internet, other people looking at it on calibrated monitors will see identical colors and brightness in the image.

If you don't calibrate your monitor, you run the risk of colors or brightness skewing to one side of the spectrum. Things might appear normal on *your* screen, but they won't look the same on other computers.

The best way to avoid this is to use a display calibration device, which is a piece of hardware that plugs in to your computer. You run its software, and it makes all of the adjustments for you (**Figure 6.1**). You can find many brands out there with different levels of calibration, but you don't need to spend a lot of money to get one that works well. If you're serious about photography, it is a necessary investment.

Figure 6.1
This is the calibration software I use for my monitors, the X-Rite ColorMunki Display (www.xrite.com). To calibrate, I launch the software and use a special device that plugs into my computer and rests on my monitor during the calibration process. You don't have to break the bank for a calibration device. Many of them are relatively inexpensive and still do a good job balancing the colors and tones of your monitor.

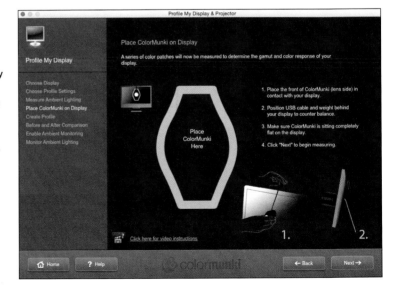

Photo-Editing Software

When it comes to processing photos on your computer, you definitely have more than one option. In this chapter, I will demonstrate how to use Adobe Photoshop Lightroom (www.adobe.com), but it's likely that you may want to consider and try some other options for postprocessing. I find that Lightroom is well rounded and allows me to process the majority of my food photographs from start to finish in just the one program, but that's not to say that I never use anything else.

One obvious alternative is Adobe Photoshop®. For those of you who do not use Lightroom, then you can still get a lot out of this chapter! Most of the techniques used here can also be applied using Adobe Bridge® and Adobe Photoshop (specifically, Adobe Camera Raw®, or ACR for short). The interfaces will look different, but the sliders and other menu names should remain the similar. Photoshop is a pixel editor, so it has some other added benefits (especially if you need to clone anything or make aggressive changes to an element in your image). The more powerful Lightroom becomes, however, the less I find myself using Photoshop.

Another application I use in conjunction with Lightroom is the on1 Perfect Photo Suite (www.on1.com). This software has many useful features, including the ability to work with layers and masking; has its own dedicated file browser to search through your folders and files; and also includes a powerful editor, Perfect Effects, where you can add color, tone, and many other types of adjustments. There are several options on the market for photography tools, and many of them offer free trials. I recommend you try them out to see which ones you prefer and go from there.

Working in Adobe Lightroom

Adobe Lightroom has seven modules that you can work from, each with their own panels, functions, and purposes. In this book, I will demonstrate how to process photos using two of these: the Library and Develop modules. The Library module is where you can import, export, and organize your photographs, and the Develop module is the place to process your RAW photos to make them stand out and look beautiful.

My Lightroom Workflow

When working in Lightroom, you will eventually develop your own methods, along with a start-to-finish workflow. I have been using Lightroom for years, and you will probably find that the order you work in is similar to my own.

Here is a typical workflow that I use in Lightroom:

1. **Import**: The first step is always to import the files into the Lightroom catalog. I typically will do this after each shoot using the memory card from my camera.

2. **Organize and sort**: Next, I sort and organize my files in the Library module. I choose which images I want to process in the Develop module, and I also organize the photos into collections if needed.

3. **Develop**: The next step is to process the photos in the Develop module. If I have multiple photos from the same shoot that are similar in exposure and subject, I will sync the develop settings for all of those images.

4. **Export**: The last step is to export my files. Most often, my photos are going to be shared on a website, so I resize them so that they are smaller (usually around 2000px wide) and export them to my hard drive.

The Library Module

One thing to keep in mind when using Lightroom is that the program first organizes a catalog of your photos in a database. All photos in Lightroom remain stored in a location and folder hierarchy of your choosing. Lightroom does not tuck your photos away in a difficult-to-reach location, buried out of sight. The Lightroom catalog only *points* to the files on your computer and shows the data from those images (the image preview, metadata, and so on). The files themselves do not relocate from where you originally saved them.

One of the biggest advantages of working in Lightroom is its ability to help you organize and catalog your photographs. This is what makes Lightroom so incredibly powerful! And all of this organization takes place in the Library module.

In this section, I will walk you through the steps for creating a catalog, importing your photographs, and also organizing your images using folders, collections, keywords, and other labels (such as flags and ratings). So, let's get started!

Creating a Catalog

When you open up Lightroom for the first time, it will typically create a default catalog on your computer. This catalog, usually named something like "Lightroom 6 Catalog.lrcat," is a good place to get started and may be the only catalog you ever need. I prefer to work with one large catalog that includes all of my photographs, and right now my Lightroom catalog has close to 250,000 files! I find that keeping all of my images organized in one catalog is the easiest way for me to work efficiently, as I am constantly jumping around to look for photos to either share online or use in articles or training materials.

Another option is to use more than one catalog. You can set this up in Lightroom by choosing **File > New Catalog**. Some reasons for multiple catalogs might be if you work with different clients and prefer to keep their work separate from all of your other images. Choosing the number of catalogs and how you ultimately organize your photographs is a matter of your own personal preference.

Importing Your Files

Now that you have your catalog, it's time to import some files! As photographers, we have to get our photos downloaded to our computers through memory cards. However, if you are new to using Lightroom or if you have some existing photos sitting on your computer, then you will probably want to import those as well. In this section, I'll show you how to do both. Let's get started with importing from a memory card, which is the one you'll likely use most often.

Importing from a Memory Card

To transfer files from your camera to your computer, you will need to use the memory card. To get started, remove the card memory card from your camera and insert it into the card reader (**Figure 6.2**). Then, in Lightroom's Library module, choose **File > Import Photos and Video**. You can also click the Import button in the lower-left portion of the window (**Figure 6.3**).

Next, the Import window pops up. There are two different views for this window: expanded and minimized. The default view is minimized, but I always recommend expanding the window to see more options. To do this, click the upside-down arrow on the bottom-left of the Import window (**Figures 6.4** and **6.5**).

Figure 6.3
Use the Import button to add photos to your Lightroom catalog.

Figure 6.2
This is the card reader I use to import files to my desktop computer, a Lexar multi-card USB reader.

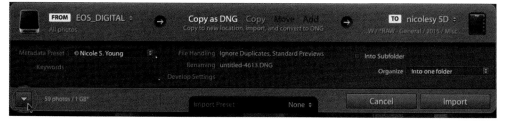

Figure 6.4
The default Import window is a smaller version with fewer options.

Figure 6.5

Figure 6.5
By expanding the
Import window,
you gain more
options to work with
when importing
your photos into
Lightroom.

Now, let's go through each of the sections within this window, starting with the Source panel on the left. The Source panel is where you select the source of your images, in this case the memory card you just inserted. Memory cards typically appear at the top of the list, so click a card's name to select it (**Figure 6.6**).

Next, go to the top of the window to choose how the image will be copied to your computer. When importing from a memory card, you have two options: Copy as DNG and Copy (**Figure 6.7**). The first option, Copy as DNG, imports the photos and then converts the RAW files to DNG files in the process. Selecting Copy copies the RAW files to your computer (CR2, NEF, and so on). If you're not sure which way to go, you might want to just stick with Copy. If you decide to convert them to DNG down the road, you can do that in the Library module under **Library > Convert Photos to DNG**.

Figure 6.6
The Source panel is
where you select the
location of the files
you want to import
into your catalog.
Here I selected a
memory card with
images photo-
graphed from my
Canon 5D Mark III.

Figure 6.7
The Copy as DNG option, which I have selected here, will import the photos and convert them to DNG files. The Copy option will directly copy your
RAW files (CR2, NEF, and so on). The other two options, Move and Add, are
only for importing photos that already exist on your hard drive and are
grayed out here because I am copying from a memory card.

What Are DNG Files?

When importing your images, you may notice that you have the option to convert your photos to DNG at the time of import. DNG stands for Digital Negative, and it is a RAW file that has a few advantages. One advantage is that this file format is nonproprietary, meaning that it is not associated with a specific brand and is less likely to be outdated in years to come.

Another great feature of the DNG file is that all of your changes are saved in the file itself. When you process a regular RAW image in Lightroom, such as a CR2 from a Canon camera, Lightroom saves a side-car file that holds all of the information from your edits (**Figure 6.8**). Without this file, the photo would be reset to its straight-out-of-the-camera state, and you would lose your changes. With a DNG file, the changes are written to the DNG file, so no additional files need to stick with the photo for the changes to appear (**Figure 6.9**).

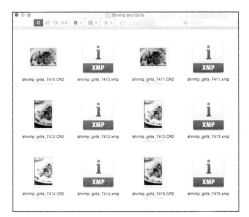

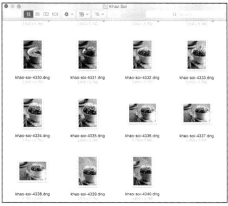

Figure 6.8
This folder is filled with Canon CR2 RAW files, along with their sidecar .XMP files. The .XMP file holds the information from changes made in the Lightroom catalog, such as white balance and tone adjustments.

Figure 6.9
With DNG files, the information from changes in the Lightroom catalog is stored inside the file.

Just below the top panel is the thumbnail preview of your images. In this section, you can select which images you want to view, how they are presented (either in a grid or as a full image), how big the thumbnails are, and also how they are sorted (**Figure 6.10**). A checkmark next to the photo means that it will be imported, and if the photo does not have a checkmark or is grayed out, it will not be imported.

Figure 6.10
The center window displays the photos you will be importing, and it also allows you to sort them and view them at different sizes.

Over on the right is where you select where to import the photos to, how you name the files, and how they are handled on import, as well as the option to add your copyright or other metadata (such as keywords) to your photos. This section can be a little bit daunting for first-time users, so let's go through each panel and discuss what it does, along with some of the basic settings you can use to get started.

- **File Handling**: Through this panel you tell Lightroom how to handle the files you are importing. For the Build Previews drop-down, I recommend sticking with the Standard setting for previews. Also leave the Smart Previews option unchecked. It's a good idea to keep a check in the Don't Import Suspected Duplicates box to prevent you from re-importing old files. If you are backing up your images to a second source, then you can deselect this box and specify the backup destination. Finally, you can place the photos into a collection on import as well.

- **File Renaming**: This panel is pretty straightforward. You choose how the files will be named. You are not required to rename them, but I prefer to give my files names that make sense. The settings I use for renaming files are to use a custom name with the original file number. For example, for this group of images I photographed a green smoothie. I will set the custom text to "smoothie," and the original file number will remain. There are other options as well, and you can even create and save your own preset. I recommend experimenting with a file-naming structure that best suits your organizational style.

- **Apply During Import**: While importing files, you also have the ability to apply certain settings to your images. If you have a develop preset you would like to apply, you can do that with the drop-down. You can also create a meta-data preset, which is a great way to embed your copyright information in the file. Last but not least, there is a box for quickly applying keywords to your files as well.

- **Destination**: The last setting is the destination where you would like your photos to reside on your computer after they are imported. Here, Lightroom gives you two options to organize your files: by date or into one folder. My preference is to create my own named folder hierarchy using the Into One Folder option, where I label my folders based on the type of photos I was creating. For food photography, that will always be the name of the dish inside a folder labeled Food.

- **Import Preset**: The last panel in the Import window is at the bottom of the window, and this is where you can save presets of your import settings. I do this often and find that it is a much faster way to quickly apply settings, and then I can make small changes (such as changing the name of the file) before importing.

  To create your own preset, first set up the Import window the way you would like to import a certain group of photos. Then, click the Import Preset drop-down and select "Save current settings as new preset." Give your preset a name and then click OK. Now, the next time you import photos, select that preset from the list, and all of your settings will be applied.

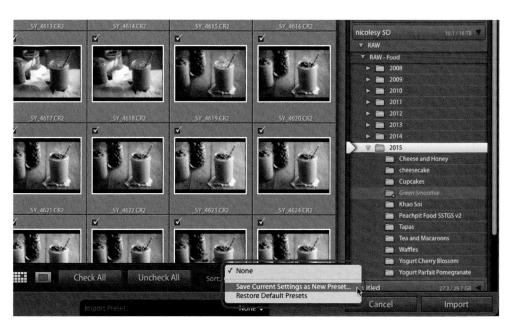

Importing from Existing Files on Your Computer

If you already have files on your computer, then importing them using the Import window is a breeze. Here's how to import existing files into your Lightroom catalog:

1. Open the Import window, and select the source files from on the left (**A**).

2. From the top, select the action you want perform with the files: Copy, Move, or Add (**B**). Copying the files makes a copy of the images and places them into a folder of your choice. Moving the files relocates the files to a new folder, and the Add option keeps the images in their existing location, which is a good choice if you already have the photos on your computer and don't want to move them. Selecting Add is the easiest and simplest option to work with; use that option for this example.

3. Because the files are being added to the catalog without being moved, you have fewer options to choose from on the right side of the window. For this example, leave the File Handling options as-is and select the appropriate settings in the Apply During Import panel (**C**).

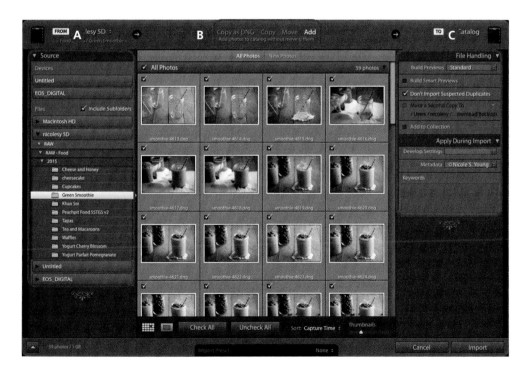

4. Click the Import button, and the photos are added to your Lightroom catalog.

Organization Tips

As I mentioned previously, one of Lightroom's most powerful features is the ability to help you stay organized. But just because you have Lightroom doesn't mean that your images will magically be filed away in an order that makes the most sense to you. It will take some planning on your part to make sure that your images are added to your catalog in an order that makes the most sense.

Folder Organization

How you ultimately organize your folders is completely up to you. Some photographers will sort their files by date (a folder for the year and then a folder for each month or day). I personally find that a bit confusing because I don't always know what or where I was photographing on a particular day of the year. Instead, I prefer to organize my folders by year, and then I list out each photo shoot within that year (**Figure 6.11**).

As you can see, I group my food photographs separate from my other files, and it's likely that you will have many other photos in your Lightroom catalog as well. Keep in mind that it may take time to decide on a structure that works best for you, so don't fret about this right away. You can even move your photos around to reorganize them, but if you do, be sure to do all of your moving from in Lightroom! Going outside of Lightroom and making changes to the folder structure will confuse Lightroom and cause it to lose track of those photos. So, if you need to rename, relocate, or reorganize your photos and folders, be sure to do it *only* from within the Folders panel in Lightroom.

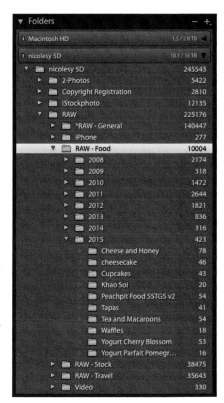

Figure 6.11
I organize the photos in my Lightroom catalog by year and then by photo shoot.

Using Collections

Staying organized using folders is a good way to maintain order in Lightroom, but you can also use the Collections panel to sort and group your photos. Saving a photo to a collection does not move the photo. Rather, it displays photos as a group, and the photos can come from any folder in your catalog.

Here are a few possibilities for collections in Lightroom:

- Your very best photos to be shared in a portfolio or gallery website

- Images that will be shared on your blog or posted to social media

- Photos to use for a specific project, such as a cookbook or eBook

- Images that you want to postprocess at a later time

- Photos to be used on a stock website

Once you have an idea for a collection, you'll need to create it. Here's how:

1. Go to the Collections panel and click the plus icon. Then, select Create Collection from the pop-up (**A**).

2. Give your collection a name, and if you have a Collection Set already created, you can add it to that as well. Also, there are a few check boxes in the Options setting to choose from. Place a check in the "Set as target collection" option, and leave the others unchecked. When you are finished, click the Create button (**B**).

3. Your new collection will now appear in the Collections panel. To add photos to it, drag and drop them from the folders in your catalog. Also, because you set this collection as a target collection, you can also use the keyboard shortcut **B** to add any selected image to that collection (**C**).

Collections, Smart Collections, and Collection Sets

When creating a new collection, you'll notice that Lightroom offers three types of collections: a collection, a smart collection, or a collection set. Here's a quick breakdown of what each of these do:

- **Collection**: This type of collection will hold photos and is the one you will use most often when using this panel. You add photos to collections manually or while you are importing your files.

- **Smart Collection**: You can create a collection that will be automatically populated based on certain criteria. For example, you could create a smart collection that shows all images you photographed in the last year that have a Pick Flag status set to Flagged. Then, Lightroom would scan through your entire catalog and automatically add those files to the folder and update it as necessary. There are many different ways you can use smart collections, and at times they can be handy.

- **Collection Set**: A collection *set* holds other collections, so you can use this to further group and organize your collections.

Selecting Keepers

After importing a batch of photos to your Lightroom catalog, odds are that you will want to process a handful of them only. The best way to know which ones you will be working on is to go through a sorting process right off the bat. Lightroom offers a few ways that you can sort through your images to select and label your best shots.

Flags, Color Labels, and Star Ratings

There are three main ways you can label your images in Lightroom: flags, color labels, and star ratings. And the great news is that you don't have to choose just one. You can, in fact, add more than one type of label to each image, so you can have different methods of sorting to organize your photos. Each sorting method can be applied either by using a keyboard shortcut or through the toolbar below the Preview window (**Figure 6.12**).

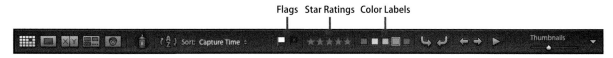

Figure 6.12
The toolbar below the Preview window allows you to sort, rate, or flag your images.

- **Flags**: Flagging is probably the simplest of the labeling methods and is the primary way I sort my images in Lightroom. Each photo can be flagged (left), unflagged (middle), or rejected (right). To flag an image (or group of images), highlight it and then press the **P** key (P stands for "pick"). You can also hover over the image and click the flag icon in the upper-left corner of the box in the Grid view or in the toolbar below the Preview window. If you would like to unflag a photo, use the keyboard shortcut **U**. And, to reject a photo, use the keyboard shortcut **X**.

- **Star Ratings**: If you prefer to rate your photos on a scale of 1 to 5, you may want to use the star ratings. To add a star rating, highlight your photo (or group of photos) and then press a number on your keypad; number 1 will give your photo a 1-star rating, 2 a 2-star rating, and so on. The highest rating you can give your images is a 5-star rating.

- **Color Labels**: Color labels are another good way to group and organize your photos. You can add red, yellow, green, blue, or purple color labels to your photos in Lightroom. I will sometimes use these as a temporary way to tell myself that I have processed the photo or want to add it to a specific collection.

Tip

Press the **T** key on your keyboard to toggle the toolbar's visibility.

Grid View vs. Loupe View

When viewing images in the Library module, you will likely view them in one of two ways: Grid view or Loupe view (**Figures 6.13** and **6.14**). In Grid view (keyboard shortcut: **G**), you can see many images at the same time, and it's the best way to label or edit several images at once. If you want to view the image closer, then press the **E** key to go to Loupe view. These options can also be selected using the toolbar below the main Preview window.

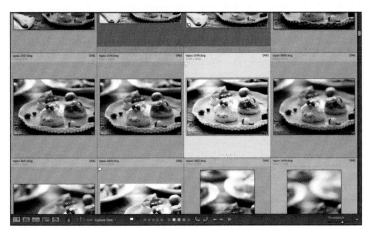

Figure 6.13
Use the Grid view (keyboard shortcut: G) to view more than one image at a time in the main window.

Figure 6.14
Use Loupe view (keyboard shortcut: E) to feature one image in the main window.

Hiding and Revealing Sidebars

You can customize the Lightroom window to display only the panels you want to view. The default window shows a left and right panel, along with a filmstrip panel at the bottom (**Figure 6.15**). However, you can toggle the visibility on all of the panels by using the keyboard shortcut Shift+Tab (**Figure 6.16**). To hide only the left and right panels, use just the Tab key. You can also hide them individually by using the small gray triangles on the far edges of the window.

Figure 6.15
This view shows all panels (top, bottom, left, and right).

Figure 6.16
Using the keyboard shortcut Shift+Tab, you can hide all panels in the Lightroom window.

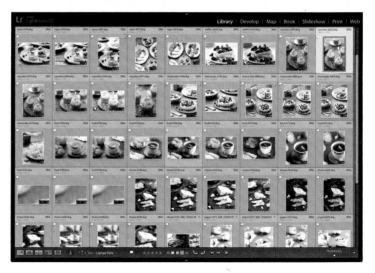

Survey Mode

If you are still trying to decide which photos to select as your keepers, you might want to consider using Survey mode. This allows you to view only select photos in a side-by-side arrangement, and it is a good way to pick your best images, especially with photos that are similar.

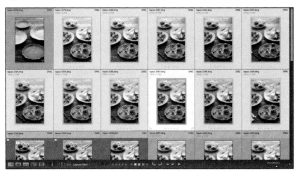

Here's how to use Survey mode in Lightroom to choose the keepers from a photo shoot:

1. Highlight a group of images using the Grid view (keyboard shortcut: **G**) in the Library module. You can hold the Shift key to select adjacent photos, or you can hold the Cmd key (PC: Ctrl) and click more than one image to highlight individual photos. (**A**)

2. Press the **N** key to enter Survey mode. Now you can see all the photos you highlighted.

3. When you find a photo you do not want to work on and want to remove from the group, hover over the image and click the X that appears in the lower-right portion of the photo. (**B**)

4. Continue X-ing out photos until you have a group of images you are happy with. (**C**)

5. When finished, press the Esc key to go back to Grid view. The photos that you selected are now the only ones highlighted, so you can apply a flag, label, or star rating to indicate that you will be processing only those files. (**D**)

Should I Delete My Rejected Files?

All photo shoots will result in photographs that you will not end up using. Maybe the composition is not ideal, or they are images you just don't like. When you run into these situations, the question to ponder is whether to delete those photos that you don't use. You could argue that if you delete them, then you would save space on your hard drive. But what if you changed your mind later?

My personal advice is to never delete your photos! Hard-drive space is cheap, and you may find a use for those images later. It's a good practice to follow *especially* when working with clients, but also for your own photos. Besides, the more experienced a photographer you become, the fewer reject photos you will end up with.

Filtering Your Picks

Once you have your images labeled, you can filter through them to show only those that you have chosen to work with. The easiest way to do this is through the filmstrip at the bottom of the window.

To sort your images, go to the far right and use the options to the right of the Filter label. You can select from the drop-down, or you can click one or more of the label items (flags, stars, or colors) to set that as your filter setting (**Figure 6.17**). (If you don't see the additional filter icons, click Filter once for them to appear.)

Figure 6.17
You can use the Filter bar to view only images with certain labels applied to them. In this example, I am filtering by flag status, but you can also use this section to filter by star rating, by color label, or by custom filter using the drop-down.

The Develop Module

Now that you have made your selections, it's time to start processing! In this section, we'll head over to the Develop module and work our way through several of the panels to give you a good idea on how to get started with processing your photos in Lightroom.

When deciding where to start editing, the best approach is to work from top to bottom. This means you will start at the topmost panel and work your way down. Of course, you can always go back and make adjustments to any panel at any time, but it's a good method to start with, especially if you are feeling overwhelmed or don't quite know what you want to do with your photo.

Cropping and Cloning

At the top of the right sidebar, just below the Histogram panel, is a row of tools. These tools can be useful when the need arises. The two you will likely use most often with food are the Crop and Spot Removal tools.

The Crop Tool

One of the first things I do with my photos before doing any processing is to crop the image (**Figure 6.18**). I do this because I like to see the overall composition of my photo

Figure 6.18
The Crop tool allows you to crop and straighten your images in Lightroom.

before making any other edits. To use the Crop tool, click the far-left icon and then use the overlay in the Preview window to make your changes with your cursor. (You can also use the keyboard shortcut **R** to activate it quickly.) Here are some things to keep in mind when cropping:

- To keep your aspect ratio locked, you can click the lock icon in the panel to prevent it from changing.

- If you would like to change the aspect ratio altogether, click the drop-down and choose one from the list or enter a custom ratio of your own.

- To straighten the image, click the Auto button above the Angle setting. If that doesn't do the trick, use the Angle slider to do it manually.

The Spot Removal Tool

If you have small spots in your image that need to be removed, such as a sensor spot or a crumb that is out of place, you can remove them using the Spot Removal tool. Here's how:

1. Zoom into your image by clicking once over the spot you want to remove. **(A)**

2. Activate the Spot Removal tool using the toolstrip, or press **Q** on your keyboard to activate it quickly.

3. Use the cursor and move the tool over the spot in your image that you would like to remove. If you need to resize the brush, you can do that from inside the panel on the right. **(B)**

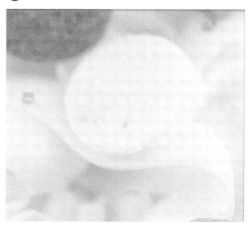

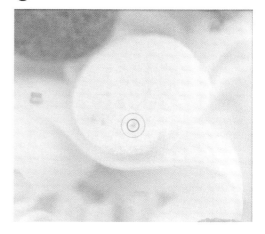

4. Next, click once over the spot, and watch it disappear! Lightroom chooses a similar area within your image to clone from, and you will see this overlay as you hover over the image. (**C**)

5. If you need to make adjustments or relocate the cloned area, hover the cursor over the circular icon until the cursor changes to a hand. Then, click and drag to a more appropriate location.

6. You can also make further adjustments to the Size, Feather, and Opacity of the cloned area inside the panel. (**D**)

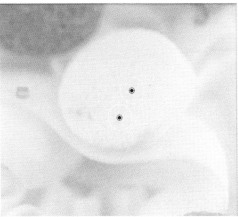

Basic Edits

Now, let's go through the panels and sliders you can use when processing the tones and color of a food photograph in the Develop module. This is a good introduction to using the panels in this module, and if you would like to see these settings in action, please turn to Chapter 7, where I show how to process several photographs from start to finish.

The Basic Panel

The Basic panel is where you will make the majority of the edits to your food photographs. It's where you can change the white balance of your raw photo, and it's also the best place to adjust the tones as well. Here is an explanation of how of these settings affect your images:

- **WB (Temp and Tint)**: This section is where you adjust the white balance of your images. Do this first before making any other changes, and try to get the photo to look as balanced as possible. It's likely that your camera did a good job, especially if you used its auto white balance, but sometimes your images will still need minor corrections. You can also try the different options in the drop-down to the right, or you can use the eyedropper tool to select a white portion of your image to automatically set the white balance based on the colors in your photo (**Figure 6.19**).

Figure 6.19
The original white balance for this image was too yellow, so I moved the Temp slider to the left to cool it down.

Previewing the Before and After Image

Sometimes the best way to know if you are on the right editing path is to see what the photo looked like before and compare it with the changes you have made. The best way to do this is by using a keyboard shortcut: the backslash key (\). Press this key to toggle the before-and-after view of your image.

- **Tone**: This section is to increase or decrease exposure and contrast in your image. When you are starting out, the best way to discover which settings to use is to just try them. Slide them back and forth until you get to a good idea of where to place the slider. You can also use the Auto button to get you off to a possible starting point and then adjust the settings from there (**Figure 6.20**).

Figure 6.20
To adjust the tone in this image, I first clicked the Auto button and then made adjustments to add more brightness and contrast.

- **Presence**: This section has three sliders: Clarity, Vibrance, and Saturation. The Clarity slider is similar to a sharpening effect. Use it lightly, or you can add a little too much "crunchiness" to your image. Both the Vibrance and Saturation sliders either increase or decrease the color in your image. Again, try to not be heavy-handed with these sliders, especially if you are going for realistic color (**Figure 6.21**).

Figure 6.21
By zooming in on this photo, you can see that I added a slight amount of clarity, along with some vibrance and saturation to enhance the colors.

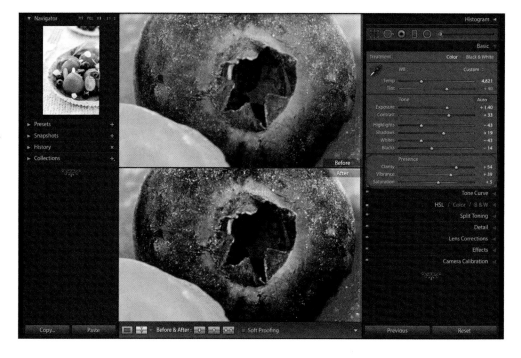

Tone Curve

The Tone Curve panel is a good place to further edit the tones in your image. You can either use the sliders in the section labeled Region or click the Point Curve icon to edit the curve yourself (**Figure 6.22**).

Figure 6.22
You can either edit the tone curve by using the sliders, like I did with this image, or you can click the small icon in the bottom right to manipulate the curve directly.

HSL

If you would like to make selective edits to the colors in your image, the HSL panel is the best place to do so. The Hue section will alter and change the colors of the image, Saturation will intensify the existing colors, and Luminance will either darken or lighten specific groups of colors (**Figure 6.23**).

Figure 6.23
For this image, I made several adjustments to make the colors stand out. I altered the Blue sliders to make them darker and more saturated, I decreased the luminance of the Yellow slider to darken the cup and the butter, and I also slightly desaturated the Orange slider to reduce some of the color in the toast.

Split Toning

With the Split Toning panel, you can alter the color of the highlights, shadows, or both. It is meant to mimic a cross-processed film photograph, and while you may not use it often with your food images, it can be a fun tool to use for other images (**Figure 6.24**).

Figure 6.24
This shows an example of a subtle split tone effect on a plate of blueberries.

Detail

The Detail panel is the place to go if you want to add sharpening or reduce the noise in your photo. My advice when using either of these sliders is to zoom in to make sure that you are not adding any artifacting or halos to the photo (**Figure 6.25**). Also, adding too much noise reduction can make the photo look "mushy." Just be aware of the changes you are making so that they are not overdone.

Lens Correction

Lightroom has the ability to correct your image for distortion and vignetting caused by certain lens types. It can also automatically remove *chromatic aberration*, which is the appearance of unsightly green or purple halos around the edges of some portions of your image (**Figure 6.26**). Chromatic aberration usually appears on photos with a lot of contrast or shiny metal objects (such as flatware) and is also more prevalent with lower-quality lenses. You can also access the other sections of this panel (Profile, Color, and Manual) to make more precise or manual adjustments to your image as needed.

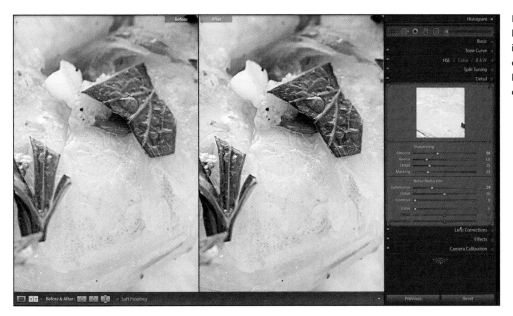

Figure 6.25
It's best to zoom in when making changes in the Detail panel to avoid overdoing it.

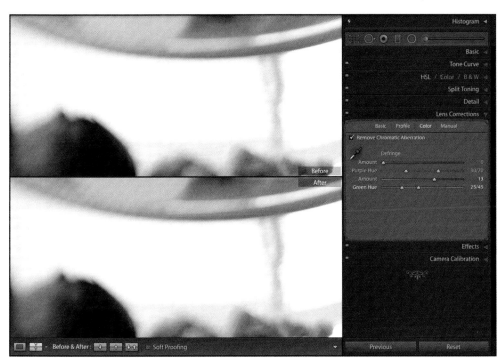

Figure 6.26
I used the Color section in the Lens Correction panel to remove green chromatic aberration from an out-of-focus portion of a photograph.

Effects

The Effects panel is for adding vignettes and film grain. It's unlikely that you will want to *add* grain to a food photograph, but you may choose to add a subtle vignette, and this is a good place to do so (**Figure 6.27**).

Figure 6.27
I added a vignette to this image to darken the edges.

Camera Calibration

The last panel in the right sidebar is Camera Calibration. Here you can select the process version (which is set to the most current version by default), as well as make adjustments to the profile (**Figure 6.28**). It is another way to adjust the colors in your image, but it's unlikely that you will find much of a need to go here regularly.

Tip

To reset any slider, hold the Opt (PC: Alt) key on your keyboard and then click over the Reset text.

Figure 6.28
Notice the difference in color saturation between the Adobe Standard profile (top) versus the Camera Landscape profile (bottom). (Note: the items listed in the Profile drop-down may vary depending on the camera model used for the photograph.)

Syncing Your Settings

When processing photos from the same food photo shoot, it's likely that you will want to copy your settings to the other images. In Lightroom this is called *syncing* your files, and you can do it easily in the Develop module. Here's how:

1. Process a photo using the panels in the Develop module.

2. Making sure that photo is selected, select (highlight) the other photos in the Filmstrip that you would like to copy the settings to.

3. Once your images are all highlighted, click the Sync button on the right. (**A**)

4. A new window pops up, asking which settings you would like to sync. It is usually best to sync only the settings that are applicable to each photo (for example, you will probably not want to sync your crop settings across all images). When you have the appropriate boxes checked, click Synchronize. (**B**)

5. All of your photos now share common settings. You may need to go through and make minor changes to some of them, but synchronizing your settings will get you to a good starting place. (**C**)

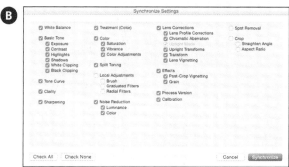

Working with Presets

One advantage to using Lightroom is that you have the ability to install and even create your own presets. A preset is a saved group of settings that can be quickly applied to any photo just by clicking it in the Presets panel on the left (**Figure 6.29**). Some reasons for creating presets are to save certain looks and styles for specific purposes (such as your website or social media) or to make it easy to quickly apply settings to your images, like a vignette or sharpening. I create and use many presets for my own work and find the Presets panel to be useful in Lightroom.

Figure 6.29
To apply a preset to a photo, just click it in the Presets panel.

Installing Presets

If you have purchased or downloaded presets from the Internet, then you can easily install them in Lightroom with just a few steps. Here's how:

1. In Lightroom's Develop module, access the Presets panel on the left.

2. In the Presets panel, create a new folder for your presets. (If you already have one you would like to use, go ahead and skip to the next step.) Right-click anywhere in the Presets panel, and choose New Folder from the context menu. (**A**) Then, give your folder a name, and click Create. (**B**)

3. Right-click the folder you just created (or whichever folder you want to use), and select Import. (**C**)

4. Navigate to the presets you downloaded (they will have the extension .lrtemplate) and highlight them. Then, click the Import button in your window (**D**). The preset will now be installed in your Lightroom catalog (**E**).

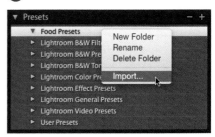

Saving Presets

If you would like to save your own preset, it's quite simple as well. Here's how:

1. Choose a processed photo that you would like to use as your preset. (**A**)

2. In the Presets panel, click the plus icon at the top of the panel. (**B**)

3. Place a check next to the items you would like to save in your new preset, and don't forget to give your preset a name. (I tend to only place checks for the panels I made changes to and always leave the White Balance and Basic Tone boxes unchecked.) When you are finished, click Create. (**C**)

   Your new preset is now saved in Lightroom. (**D**)

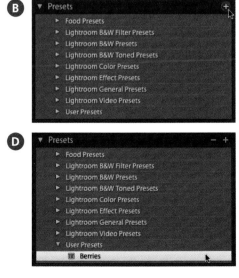

Exporting Your Files

When you are ready to share, publish, or print your photographs, you will need to export the processed files. And while the export function takes place in the Library module, it is an important enough feature to warrant its own section within this chapter. So let's get started and walk through each of the steps to take when exporting photographs from Lightroom.

Prepping for Export

The first step in exporting files is to decide which image or group of images you would like to export. This requires you to be in the Library module, and I prefer to be in Grid view for this, especially when batch-exporting my photos.

Let's say I want to export three photos to share on my blog. I will highlight each photo and then either go to **File > Export** in the menu or click the Export button on the bottom-left portion of the window (**Figure 6.30**).

Figure 6.30
To export a file or group of files, highlight them and then click the Export button.

The Export Window

After you initiate the export process, a new window appears giving you a fair number of options to choose from (**Figure 6.31**). Let's walk through each of these steps one at a time so that you can familiarize yourself with each setting:

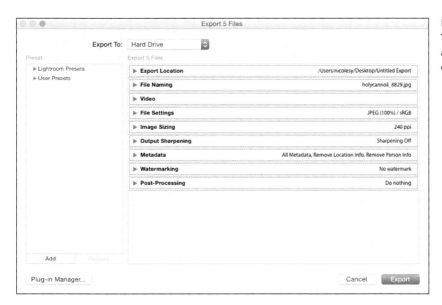

Figure 6.31
The Export window in Lightroom allows you to fully customize the export process.

- **Export To**: This setting allows you to specify the platform to which you will export the file. The majority of the time you will select Hard Drive as your option, and this is the option I choose every time I export from this window. If you have any plug-ins installed into Lightroom, then you may see those appear here as well.

- **Export Location**: The location is the folder destination your files will be saved in after exporting. In the "Export to" drop-down, you have three main options: "Specific folder," "Choose folder later," and "Same folder as original photo." If I know exactly where I want the photo to go (and I usually do), then I select "Specific folder."

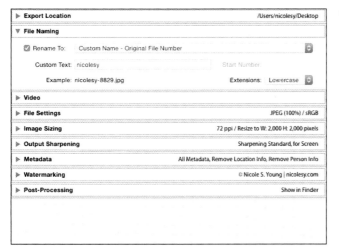

- **File Naming**: If you would like to rename your files, then this is the place to do so. You can choose from any of the naming templates in the drop-down, and you can also create and save your own template.

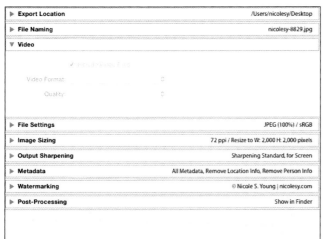

- **Video**: This section is for exporting video files. To use, place a check next to the Include Video Files box, and select your video format and quality. If you are exporting still photographs only, like I am with this example, then this section will be grayed out.

- **File Settings**: Here you select the file format in which your image will be exported (JPEG, PSD, TIFF, DNG, or Original), the color space (sRGB, Adobe RGB, ProPhoto RGB, or your own), and also the quality on a scale of 1 to 100. You are also able to limit the file size by placing a value (in kilobytes) and the file size will stay within those parameters.

- **Image Sizing**: If you would like to make your image smaller than its original dimensions, then you will use this section to set the size you want your image to be after it is exported. You can set it in pixels, inches, or centimeters, as well as the resolution.

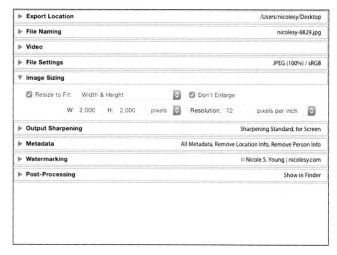

- **Output Sharpening**: You can use this section to add sharpening to your image as it is exported. The settings here are determined by how you will share your photo: on a screen (websites, slideshows, and so on) or printed on either matte or glossy paper.

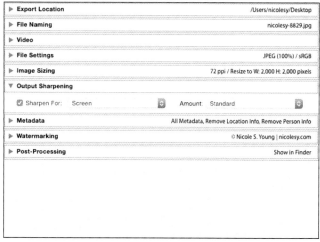

- **Metadata**: Here you can set how much metadata is included with your image in the exported file. This is a good setting to use if you would like to hide certain things, such as the GPS coordinates, camera info, or keywords that include people's names.

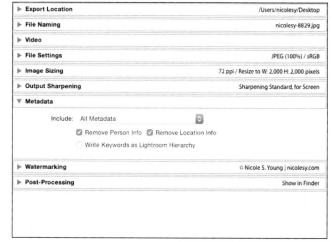

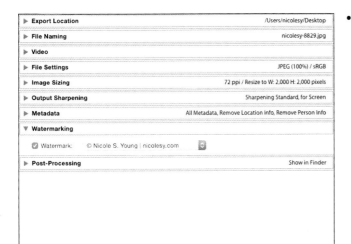

- **Watermarking**: This is a good place to add a visible watermark to your image. You can access a separate window where you can customize and configure the watermark as either a logo or text, and even the positioning of the watermark on your image. The Watermark Editor also allows you to add either an image (JPEG or PNG) or a text watermark to be applied to your exported photos.

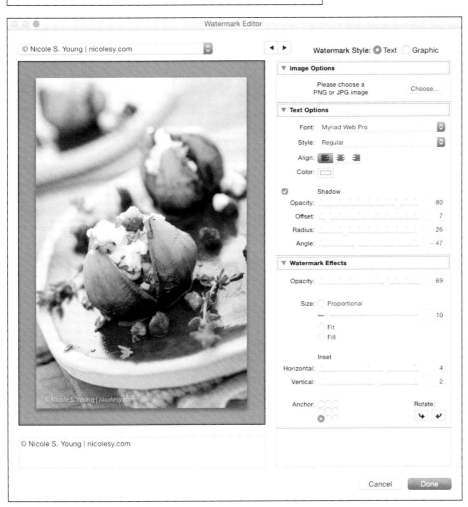

- **Post-Processing**: This setting allows you to continue working on your image in another application or just view the photo in the folder, after the file is exported.

When all of the options are set appropriately, click the Export button in the bottom right, and Lightroom will export the images to your computer.

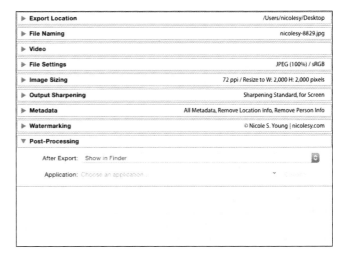

Working with Export Presets

On the left portion of the Export window is a section for presets. These presets, just like the ones in the Develop module, allow you to save settings and quickly apply them to images you export in the future. They are a great way to speed up your processing time and also help you to not forget anything important when exporting for a specific purpose, such as to print at a certain size or to publish in your portfolio.

Creating an export preset is simple:

1. Apply your settings in the Export window, but don't export the photos quite yet.

2. In the Preset panel, click the Add button. (**A**)

3. A window pops up allowing you to name your preset and also to select a folder (or create a new one). Make your settings, and click Create. (**B**)

Now your Preset is visible in the Preset panel for you to use on other images. (**C**)

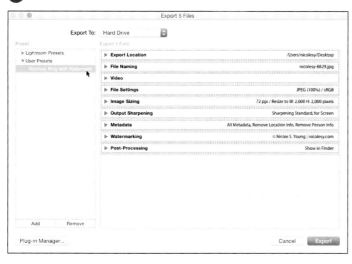

Chapter 6 Challenges

Now it's time to put what you've learned in this chapter to the test!

Import Photos into Lightroom

Locate a group of photos, either from a memory card used in a recent photo shoot or from photos already existing on your computer, and import them into your Lightroom catalog. Be sure to use the expanded view so that you can customize the import settings as much as possible. Before you import the photos, create an import preset to use on other images down the road.

Sort and Organize Your Images

In the Library module, sort through a folder of images to find the best shots. Use the flags or other rating system to label your photos, and try using the Survey mode for shots that are similar. You can also create a new collection for your favorite shots and start adding images to that as well.

Process a Batch of Photos

Find a group of photos that are similar and process one of them using the Develop module. Then, when you are finished, synchronize the settings so that all of the changes are applied to every image in the group. If you want to save those settings to use on other images, save a preset in the Presets panel on the left side of the Develop module.

Export a Photo for Web Use

When you have a photo that is ready to share online, export it using the Export window. Resize the photo so that it is a good size for sharing (I usually set mine to 2000px on the longest side at 72ppi), and feel free to add output sharpening. When you have your settings in place, save them as an export preset so that you can use them for other images in the future.

Share your results with the book's Flickr group! Join the group here: flickr.com/groups/ foodphotographyfromsnapshotstogreatshots

Canon 70D · ISO 250 ·
1/40 sec. · f/4.5 ·
Canon EF-S 24mm lens

7

Behind the Scenes

Photographing Food from Start to Finish

Seeing a finished photograph and looking at a lot of images of food are great ways to learn how to improve your photography or maybe just become inspired. But watching *how* the images were made can be even more helpful. In this chapter, you will see "behind the scenes" of creating four images. I'll start with the styling, props, and lighting, and then I will walk you through the editing process in Adobe Lightroom.

I randomly dropped berries in the background to add some depth and messiness to the scene.

When I find myself eating something regularly, it usually ends up as a subject in one of my food photographs. This was the case with this green mango smoothie. I often add berries and other fruit to the blender to make a nice, healthy snack but sometimes opt for a more sweet tropical fruit, such as mango. The added benefit of using mangoes is that they make the color of the smoothie bright green, which makes it really "pop" in the photograph.

Canon 5D Mark III •
ISO 100 • 0.3 sec. •
f/2.8 • Canon 100mm
f/2.8L Macro lens

I spritzed the blueberries with canned water to make them look fresher.

A small piece of cheese-cloth helps add a barrier between the glass and the textured tabletop.

Poring Over the Picture

I added additional salads in the background in a light textured bowl to add depth without being too overwhelming.

An intricate fork and small white napkin add a nice touch of realism to the setup.

Because of their diversity and unlimited options for color and texture, salads are a fun subject to photograph. For this image, I decided to create a healthy grapefruit salad. Grapefruit is a beautiful citrus fruit, with bright texture and color, and it wasn't difficult to make it look gorgeous. I did, however, add mint and pomegranate seeds to the dish for some diversity, and I paired the salad with a light blue tablecloth, which complemented the pink color of the grapefruit.

The scene was backlit, which helped brighten up both the mint and translucent grapefruit segments.

Canon 5D Mark III •
ISO 100 • 1 sec. •
ƒ/5.6 • Canon 100mm
ƒ/2.8L Macro lens

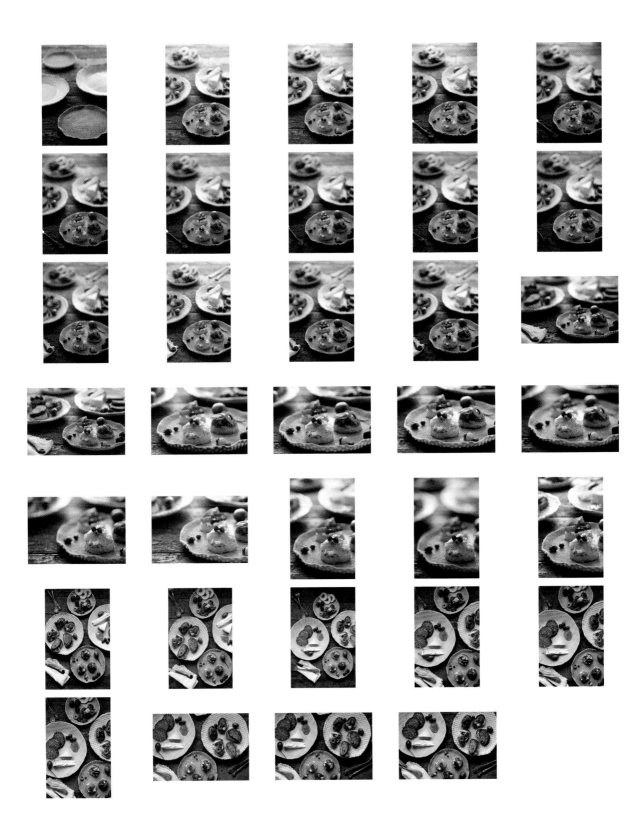

Appetizers

When photographing food for a particular purpose, such as a book or a specific layout, you may find a few challenges added to your setup. Maybe you need to compose the scene a certain way, use specific ingredients, or photograph it so that it fits inside of an exact crop ratio. These added challenges require you to be much more deliberate with your photo shoot.

For example, I decided to create a photograph specifically for the cover of this book. The cover design had to match the rest of the *Snapshots to Great Shots* series, so I had little say with where the main title text was positioned. Because of that I really had to plan out the type of food, its composition, and also where each element would be placed for it to be a good fit for the cover design.

The biggest challenge I had with this shoot was making sure that the focal point was low in the frame. For many of my photographs, the focal point is along a third-line or even close to the center of the image. If I had stuck to that way of photographing for the cover, however, then the focal point would have been hidden by the title of the book.

To create an ideal setup, I knew that I needed a scene where the main focal point was close to the bottom edge of the image. Because of that, I decided to photograph food that was small and also to compose it so that the entire main subject fit in the bottom third of the frame. This is how I came up with the idea to create small, finger-food appetizers for the cover shot (**Figures 7.1** and **7.2**).

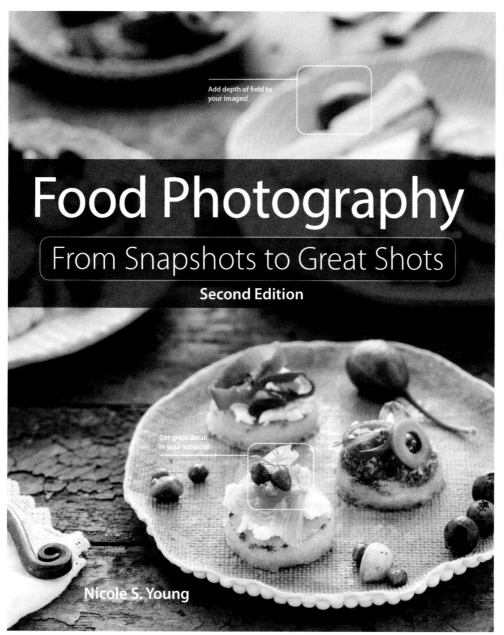

Figure 7.2
The image fits beautifully in the book cover template, with enough room for the title at the top.

Add depth of field to your images!

Food Photography

From Snapshots to Great Shots

Second Edition

Get great detail in your subjects!

Nicole S. Young

Props and Styling

The most important aspect of this photograph was that it would look good as a cover image for my book. The composition was extremely important, and I needed to make sure that I could fit all of the items inside of a vertical orientation. So the first thing that I did was to try a mock-up without the actual food. I selected my props, set up all of the plates inside of the frame, and positioned everything so that it was nice and balanced (**Figure 7.3**).

Figure 7.3
I positioned all of the plates on the table to compose my shot before preparing the food.

Canon 5D Mark III · ISO 100 · 1/6 sec. · ƒ/4.5 · Canon 100mm ƒ/2.8L Macro lens

For this shoot, I decided to go with a painted wood tabletop. I knew that I would be getting in close with my macro lens, which would emphasize the beautiful textured surface and add an extra element of depth to the photo.

In terms of dishes, I tend to prefer to use circular plates for my food photographs, especially when adding more than one plate in the scene. This setup was no exception. By using circular plates I was able to stagger them side by side without any odd angles going in strange directions, which could be a distracting element in the photo. I also chose from my handmade plates.

As a small touch, I added a simple white napkin in the corner and placed a utensil on it (**Figure 7.4**). You can't tell from the photograph, but it's a cheese spreader, but with careful placement it can stand in for any type of flatware. In some of the other frames (particularly when photographing from overhead), I added some additional flatware to balance the scene (**Figure 7.5**).

Figure 7.4
I added a simple napkin and utensil in the left corner of the frame.

Canon 5D Mark III · ISO 100 · 1/8 sec. · ƒ/5.6 · Canon 100mm ƒ/2.8L Macro lens

Figure 7.5
Additional flatware was added for the overhead shots to balance the composition.

Canon 5D Mark III • ISO 100 • 0.7 sec • ƒ/11 • Canon 100mm ƒ/2.8L Macro lens

To style the food for this scene, I decided to go with a variety of different types of appetizers. The primary subject in this photograph is a small polenta cake, cut into a tiny bite-size portion, lightly pan-fried, and then topped with goat cheese, smoked salmon, some capers, and a sprig of dill. I also added two other polenta cakes to the same plate and topped them with other varieties of items (cheese, pesto, pickled peppers, and olives). Then, to make the plate look fuller, I placed some other items on it (capers, blueberries, garlic, and a caper berry).

For the other plates in the background, I added completely different finger foods to add dimension to the image. One of the plates contained cheeses and peppered salami, another contained crostini with varied toppings, and in the far background I piled up some miscellaneous ingredients (pickled peppers, tomatoes, watermelon radishes, and raspberries). I was not as concerned with the specific styling of the background plate because I knew that it would be out of focus for the main cover image.

Lighting Setup

For this image, as with all of the images you will see in this chapter, I opted to use window light. I do my food photography in my office and have a small space beneath a window as my dedicated shooting space. For this photo I wanted the light to glow behind the food and also be lit evenly across the scene, so I chose to backlight it with the window behind the setup (**Figure 7.6**).

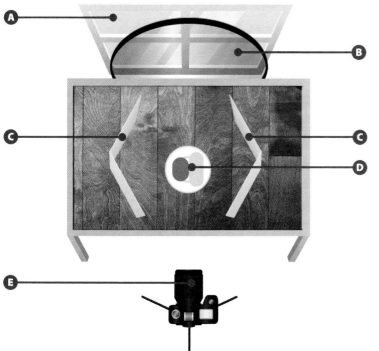

Figure 7.6
This lighting diagram shows the behind-the-scenes setup of the cover image.

A Window light
B Diffuser panel
C Folded foam board
D Appetizers
E Canon 5D Mark III

The light coming through the window was bright, so I diffused it with two Tri-Grip diffusers. I also wanted to fill in some of the shadows and bounce the light back into the scene, so I placed a folded white foam board on either side of the setup (**Figure 7.7**). A foamboard reflector like this does two things: It brightens up the image (fewer shadows and dark areas), and it also evens out the light so that the background is not overly bright. I also placed pieces of white foam board against the window on either side of the diffusers to prevent any bright light from leaking into the sides of the image.

After I worked with this setup for several minutes to get a good cover image, I decided to change up my composition and capture some additional frames. One variation was an overhead shot of the food, but to take it I needed to work with a table that was lower to the ground. The shooting table I use has two levels, and one of them is about the height of a coffee table, so I lowered my entire setup in relation to that. I also repositioned my tripod so that it partially rested on the tabletop, which allowed me to point my camera straight down on the food (**Figure 7.8**).

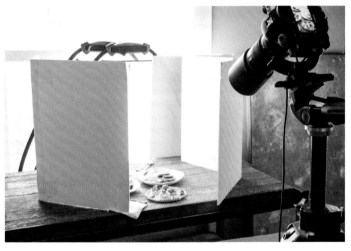

Figure 7.7
Here is a photograph of the first setup in action.

Canon 5D 70D · ISO 640 · 1/40 sec. · *f*/4.5 · Canon EF-S 24mm lens

Figure 7.8
This behind-the-scenes setup for taking overhead images illustrates the lowered table and repositioned tripod.

Canon 5D 70D · ISO 250 · 1/40 sec. · *f*/4.5 · Canon EF-S 24mm lens

By the time the shoot-down setup was ready, the light outside had become a little less bright, so I no longer needed to use the diffusers. The table is also lower than the window, so while it does get sufficient light, it is usually not as intense as when I use the taller table. I did, however, keep one of the folded white foam boards to the left of the food to bounce light back onto the scene.

Postprocessing

Now let's go through the steps to process this photo in Lightroom.

Step 1: Open the Image in the Lightroom Develop Module

First, I select the photo and click the keyboard shortcut D to open it in the Lightroom Develop module.

Step 2: Edit Tone Settings in the Basic Panel

When I process images in Lightroom, the first panel I work from is the Basic panel, and I often start from the top and work my way down. This photo already has good white balance out of the camera, so there is no need to adjust that setting. However, it is a little bit dark (especially toward the bottom of the frame), so I will first adjust the settings in the Tone section of the Basic panel.

To make the image brighter and have more contrast, I increase the Exposure to +0.45. I also decrease the Highlights and Whites sliders to remove some of the hot spots in the photo (both are set to –10), as well as increase Shadows to +43 and Blacks to +15 to bring out the detail in the darker areas.

Step 3: Add Vibrance and Saturation to Intensify the Colors

Next, at the bottom of the Basic panel, I use the Vibrance and Saturation sliders to intensify the colors in the scene by setting them both to +15.

Step 4: Adjust the Tone Curve

The image is still lacking the contrast I want, so I add this in the Tone Curve panel. I go down to the Point Curve setting and select Strong Contrast from the drop-down. Then, I adjust the settings to decrease both the bright areas, as well as brighten the dark areas: Highlights to –12, Lights to –11, Darks to +12, and Shadows to +33.

Step 5: Add a Gradient

The top of the photo is still a little too bright for my taste, so in this last step I want to darken just that area. To do this, I will use the Gradient tool. I select it at the top and click and drag from the top of the image all the way to the bottom while holding the Shift key to keep it straight. Then, I set the Exposure setting to –0.66 to darken the top portion of the image.

Green Mango Smoothie

I am in love with smoothies. I have one almost every day, and it's my way of sneaking a few servings of leafy green vegetables into my diet. Depending on the other ingredients added to the smoothie, spinach (which is what I use most often) can make the smoothie look brown or muddy-colored. However, when I use bright fruits, such as mangos and bananas, it keeps the green color intact and makes it bright and beautiful—and much more photogenic!

Props and Styling

For this photo, I wanted to showcase the smoothie and set it up with a few other glasses filled in the background. I also wanted to use a clear glass so that the smoothie was visible through the cup. And, because I like to drink my smoothies with a straw, I added green straws that I had in my prop closet.

My first step was to set up the glasses and frame the shot (**Figure 7.9**). Because this was a simple setup, I chose a highly textured wooden surface for the tabletop. I added a small piece of cheesecloth below the "hero" glass to help bring the attention to that specific smoothie. The cheesecloth also served as separator between the glass and the surface; I often like to place textiles between dishes and the tabletop to give it more depth and texture.

Figure 7.9
To set up the composition for this photo, I started by positioning the glass cups on the table.

Canon 5D Mark III ·
ISO 100 · 1/4 sec. ·
f/2.8 · Canon 100mm
f/2.8L Macro lens

Once I framed everything up and fired off a few test shots, I blended the smoothie and brought it over to the set. I wanted to make sure that I did not drip any of it onto the tabletop, so I placed paper towels around the cups and then used a spoon to fill up the first cup (**Figure 7.10**). It's a good thing I did, because I dripped a little bit. Paper towels to the rescue!

One of the garnishes that I had on hand was fresh blueberries. That was lucky, because after I filled the first and second cup with the smoothie, I realized I did not have enough for the third! Instead, I decided to fill the third cup with fresh blueberries. Then I started adding them to the tops of the smoothies to provide height and color contrast. I also put a few sprigs of mint behind the blueberries, which added texture to the tops of the smoothie (**Figure 7.11**). For added freshness, I spritzed the blueberries with some canned water to make them look even more appealing.

Next, I wanted to add an element of natural (or even controlled) messiness, so I decided to drop blueberries onto the table all around the glasses. This helped keep the space from looking too sparse and also added more interest into the background of the photos. I first dropped them randomly but then would rearrange a few as needed to ensure proper placement for each photograph (**Figure 7.12**).

Figure 7.10
I placed paper towels around the glasses before adding the smoothie to catch drips and spills.

Canon 5D Mark III • ISO 100 • 1/8 sec. • ƒ/2.8 • Canon 100mm ƒ/2.8L Macro lens

Figure 7.11
I used blueberries and mint to garnish the tops of the smoothies.

Canon 5D Mark III •
ISO 100 • 0.3 sec. •
ƒ/2.8 • Canon 100mm
ƒ/2.8L Macro lens

Figure 7.12
To add an element of natural messiness, I dropped blueberries all over the tabletop.

Canon 5D Mark III •
ISO 100 • 0.5 sec. •
ƒ/4 • Canon 100mm
ƒ/2.8L Macro lens

Lighting Setup

For this setup, I decided to sidelight the scene. Glass surfaces can be reflective and difficult to work with, and by using sidelighting I was able to prevent unwanted glares and reflections from showing up on the glass. To help reduce glare even further, I used my standard, large, 4'6" diffuser next to the window to soften the light (**Figures 7.13** and **7.14**).

There was a good shadow on the left side of the glass, which was not entirely displeasing (**Figure 7.15**). To give myself some options, however, I used a silver reflector on the left to bounce the light back in and brighten up the scene (**Figure 7.16**). Both images were acceptable, but sometimes it is nice to have a few different styles of lighting to work with when viewing the final images on the computer.

Figure 7.13
Here is the behind-the-scenes setup for this shot.

Fuji X-T1 · ISO 640 ·
1/100 sec · ƒ/2.0 ·
Zeiss 32mm ƒ/1.8 lens

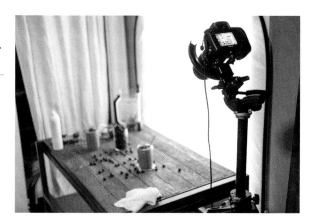

Figure 7.14
This lighting diagram shows my plan for the shot.
A Window light
B Diffuser panel
C Smoothie
D Canon 5D Mark III

Figure 7.15
I did not use a reflector for this image.
....
Canon 5D Mark III •
ISO 100 • 0.7 sec. •
ƒ/4 • Canon 100mm
ƒ/2.8L Macro lens

Figure 7.16
I used a silver reflector to bounce light into the left side of this image.
....
Canon 5D Mark III •
ISO 100 • 0.7 sec. •
ƒ/4 • Canon 100mm
ƒ/2.8L Macro lens

Last but not least, another technique I played around with was the depth of field. I was not quite sure how blurred I wanted the background, and so I photographed the scene at different aperture levels to give myself some options later. The tiny preview image on the back of the camera does a great job of giving instant feedback, but it can sometimes be misleading for previewing the blur in the background. So for this image, I photographed several of the setups at two different apertures: one at a wide aperture (*f*/2.8) to give it a blurred background and one at a smaller aperture (*f*/6.7) to see more detail in the background (**Figures 7.17** and **7.18**).

Figure 7.17
I used a wide aperture (*f*/2.8) to blur the background of this photo.

Canon 5D Mark III • ISO 100 • 0.3 sec. • *f*/2.8 •
Canon 100mm *f*/2.8L Macro lens

Figure 7.18
To show more detail in the background, I used a more narrow aperture (*f*/6.7).

Canon 5D Mark III • ISO 100 • 2 sec. • *f*/6.7 •
Canon 100mm *f*/2.8L Macro lens

Postprocessing

Now let's go through the steps to process this photo in Lightroom.

Step 1: Open the Image in the Lightroom Develop Module

First, I select the photo and click the keyboard shortcut D to open it up into the Lightroom Develop module.

Step 2: Adjust the White Balance

Next, I go into the White Balance settings at the top of the Basic panel. This image looks like it could use a little bit of warmth, so I increase the temperature to 5100.

Step 3: Brighten the Image with Tone Adjustments

Now I will use the Tone settings to brighten the image. First, I click the Auto button to see what Lightroom thinks I should adjust, and it does a pretty good job. I would like to remove some of the dark shadows from the lower-left portion of the photo, however, so to do that I increase the Shadow slider to +50.

Step 4: Intensify the Colors with the Vibrance Slider

I want to slightly intensify the colors of the photo, but I need to be careful not to overdo it. When working with an image with a lot of green, it can be easy to make the green colors look too oversaturated. I increase the Vibrance slider to +20 to add a nice subtle burst of color without making the green look unrealistic.

Step 5: Add a Vignette

Now, I want to slightly darken the edges of the photo, and the easiest way to do this is with a vignette. In the Effects panel, I use the Post-Crop Vignetting section to apply my vignette. I set Amount to −10, Midpoint to 0, and Feather to 100. Then, in the top right of this panel, I change the Style to Paint overlay to make the effect a little more subtle.

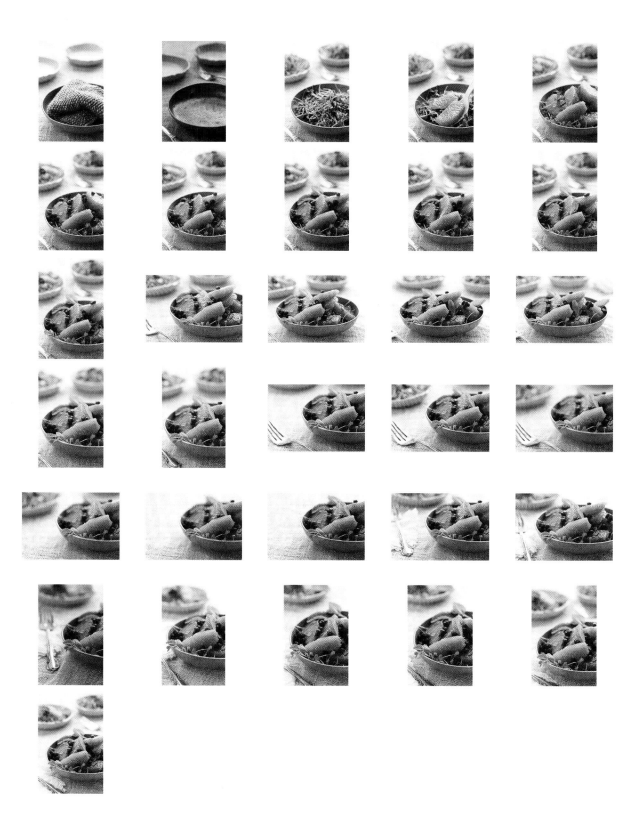

Grapefruit Salad

Many of the photographs you will see me make are of foods that I love to eat. Because the work I do is for my stock portfolio and not for clients, I have the luxury of being able to photograph anything I like. Because of that, most of the time the food that appears in front of my camera is there because I decided to have it for lunch.

This photograph of a grapefruit salad is no exception. I did, however, get the inspiration from a photo I found in a magazine of a simple grapefruit-mint salad. Because I find myself eating more and more red grapefruit, integrating it into my food photographs made sense as well.

Props and Styling

Just as I do with every other food setup, I started by selecting the dishes and tabletop I would use for this photograph. Because the grapefruit was a soft pink color, I wanted to go with colors that would help it stand out. So, I decided to place a light blue scarf over the entire table to mimic the look of a tablecloth.

For the dishes, my first instinct was to use my favorite small metal dish that I use quite often. It is a shallow bowl, which was what I was looking for so that I could pile up the grapefruit without them sliding around but also so that I could see what was in the bottom of the dish. I also wanted to place some bowls in the background, and I needed similar sized dishes to make the setup look balanced. So, I chose two of my handmade ceramic dishes, each with a mint-colored glaze to help blend better with the background.

When I photograph food that will be eaten a certain way, I always make sure that I have a relevant utensil to go along with it. In this case, I needed a fork, and because I was using a simple bowl for the foreground image, I was able to complement it with a more intricately decorated fork. I also added a napkin into some of the later shots to add a little bit more depth to the image (**Figure 7.19**).

Next, I needed to create the salad. When working with food with different elements pieced together, like with a salad or a pasta dish, I always create the salad differently than the way I would make it if I were eating it. When I make a salad to eat, I put all of the ingredients in a bowl, toss them together, and then put a portion of it on a plate to eat. When I am photographing salads, however, I place every item in the bowl or plate individually, gently layering them so that they don't get messy and damaged from being mixed around in a bowl.

Figure 7.19
I added a fork and napkin to the lower-left corner of the frame to balance the composition.

Canon 5D Mark III •
ISO 100 • 0.7 sec. •
ƒ/5.6 • Canon 100mm
ƒ/2.8L Macro lens

For this salad, I placed each of the four ingredients one at a time. I started with the microgreens and put a good amount at the bottom of each dish (**Figure 7.20**). Then, I segmented the grapefruit to remove the pith and keep the grapefruit beautiful with no cut marks, added some sliced and whole-leaf mint (**Figure 7.21**), and topped everything with some pomegranate seeds (**Figures 7.22** and **7.23**). Each element was placed carefully and deliberately, and items in the foreground were handpicked so that the more beautiful pieces were up front, particularly with the more prominent wedge of grapefruit and mint garnish (**Figure 7.24**).

Figure 7.20
To style the dish, first I added the microgreens to the bottom of each bowl.

Canon 5D Mark III · ISO 100 · 1 sec. · *f*/5.6 ·
Canon 100mm *f*/2.8L Macro lens

Figure 7.21
Next, I carefully placed each grapefruit segment into the dishes.

Canon 5D Mark III · ISO 100 · 1 sec. · *f*/5.6 ·
Canon 100mm *f*/2.8L Macro lens

Figure 7.22

I wanted a little bit more brightness, so I added some sliced mint and mint leaves to the top of the grapefruit.

Canon 5D Mark III · ISO 100 · 1 sec. · ƒ/5.6 ·
Canon 100mm ƒ/2.8L Macro lens

Figure 7.23

To finish off the food styling, I placed pomegranate seeds to garnish the dishes.

Canon 5D Mark III · ISO 100 · 1/8 sec. · ƒ/5.6 ·
Canon 100mm ƒ/2.8L Macro lens

Figure 7.24
This is my food styling setup, with each item organized in a separate prep bowl. I do this so that I can easily find the most beautiful elements to place in the scene.

iPhone 6 Plus · ISO 125 · 1/15 sec. · f/2.2 · Focal length (full-frame equivalent): 29mm

For the bowls in the background, I wanted to repeat the same dish, so I created those salads at the same time as the main salad in the front. However, because I knew that those dishes would be "background only" and would likely be out of focus, I was not as selective or particular about how they looked. I am, however, always aware of what is happening in the background and will move items in the dish around to balance the colors or composition so that it blends well with the main subject of the photograph.

Lighting Setup

For this image, I decided to go with backlighting. I knew that I would be using a mint garnish, and backlighting can help make the garnishes "glow" and be bright (the light shines through the leaves). I also wanted to add some highlight to the tops of the grapefruit segments and let the light shine through its slightly translucent pulp (**Figure 7.25**).

Before I photographed the scene with food, I first set up all of the bowls and did a test shot. Rather than use empty bowls, however, I like to add some type of stand-in substance to help with the composition and lighting. So, I grabbed a knitted cloth that I had nearby that was similar in color to the grapefruit, placed it in the bowl, focused the camera, and then fired off a test shot (**Figure 7.26**). Usually, I am looking for basic light and composition at this point, just so that I don't have an enormous amount of work to do when I actually have the food on set.

Because this image is backlit, I needed to make sure that the light coming from behind was not too overpowering. To prevent this from happening, I softened the light with two

Figure 7.25
By backlighting the food, I was able to add a subtle glow to both the mint and the grapefruit segments.

Canon 5D Mark III • ISO 100 • 1 sec. • ƒ/5.6 • Canon 100mm ƒ/2.8L Macro lens

Figure 7.26
I used a napkin as a stand-in when setting up the lighting for this image.

Canon 5D Mark III • ISO 100 • 1.5 sec. • ƒ/5.6 • Canon 100mm ƒ/2.8L Macro lens diffusers: one large diffuser (4'6") and one Tri-Grip diffuser. I also placed a piece of foam board at the base of the table so that it was covering about 8 inches of the background. This helped keep the light from being too overwhelmingly bright in the background of the image. Then, I added a single, folded piece of foam board to the left of the image to bounce light in on the left, and during each shot I used a hand-held silver reflector to fill the front and right side of the image with some reflected light (**Figures 7.27** and **7.28**).

Figure 7.27
This is the behind-the-scenes view of this photograph.

Fuji X-T1 • ISO 500 • 1/100 sec. • ƒ/1.8 •
Zeiss 32mm ƒ/1.8 lens

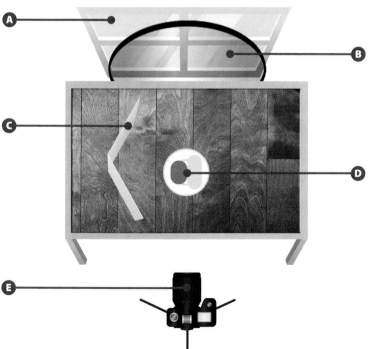

Figure 7.28
This lighting diagram illustrates how I set up this shot.

A Window light
B Diffuser panel
C Folded foam board
D Grapefruit salad
E Canon 5D Mark III

Postprocessing

Now let's go through the steps to process this photo in Lightroom.

Step 1: Open the Image in the Lightroom Develop Module

First, I select the photo and click the keyboard shortcut D to open it up into the Lightroom Develop module.

Step 2: Adjust the White Balance

The image looks a little cool, so I will warm it up using the White Balance setting in the Basic panel. Specifically, I increase the Temperature slider to 6050. This makes a subtle change, but it is always best to get the white balance to your precise liking so that other changes amplify the proper colors in the photo.

Step 3: Brighten the Image with the Tone Section

Next, I turn my attention to the Tone section. First, I click the Auto button to see what it does to the photo. It did a good job, but I still want to intensify the bright areas of the scene. So, I increase the Whites slider to +37. I also increase the Shadows slider to +22 to brighten up some of the dark areas as well.

Step 4: Increase Contrast with the Tone Curve

Now I want to add some contrast to the image using the Tone Curve. To do this, I simply select the Medium Contrast setting from the Point Curve drop-down.

Step 5: Adjust the Color Luminosity

In the HSL panel, I click Luminance at the top to make some adjustments to specific colors in the scene. First, I increase the Red slider to +21, which brightens up the grapefruit segments and pomegranate seeds. Then, I decrease the Aqua and Blue sliders to –65, which slightly darkens the blue cloth and plates in the background.

Step 6: Add a Gradient

In this last step, I would like to darken the top portion of the image so that the tones are balanced with the rest of the photo. I activate the Gradient tool at the top and then click at the top of the photo and drag it down near the bottom. Then, I set Exposure to –0.29 and Highlights to –53.

Khao Soi

While on a trip to Chiang Mai, Thailand, I ordered Khao Soi at a local restaurant and immediately fell in love (**Figure 7.29**). It was creamy, spicy, crunchy, and also colorful! As soon as I ate it that first time I knew that I would need to find a recipe and photograph it after I got home. And sure enough, I did!

Figure 7.29
This image, photographed at a restaurant in Chiang Mai, Thailand, represents what traditional Khao Soi looks like.

Fuji X-T1 · ISO 1250 · 1/125 sec. · ƒ/3.6 · Fuji 18–55mm ƒ/2.8–4 lens

Props and Styling

Before I set up this scene, I had an idea in my head of what it would look like. I had a bowl in mind, as well as a tabletop. So, I set everything up and did a few test shots but immediately realized that the color (particularly with the tabletop) was too orange (**Figures 7.30** and **7.31**). The soup itself is a bright orange color, and I didn't want to overdo it with that one color. Instead, I opted for a nice rustic tabletop (the same table surface used on the cover of this book) so that I had a more neutral color to work with and the soup would be the star of the scene (**Figure 7.32**).

Figure 7.30
I started with a wooden bowl and a rust-colored background. What I thought I wanted to use for my props added up to be too orange.

Canon 5D Mark III • ISO 100 • 2 sec. • ƒ/5.6 •
Canon 100mm ƒ/2.8L Macro lens

Figure 7.31
I switched out the bowl, thinking that a different bowl might help, but the overall colors in the scene were still much too warm for my liking.

Canon 5D Mark III • ISO 100 • 1 sec. • ƒ/5.6 •
Canon 100mm ƒ/2.8L Macro lens

In terms of props, I wanted to use a wooden bowl and eventually decided on a small, light-colored bowl. Because many of the garnishes used on this dish were small, the bowl I chose helped make them more prominent and visible in the photograph. I repeated the wooden elements in the background (a small plate and soup spoon) to balance out the composition of the scene. I also placed a small piece of cheesecloth beneath the bowl, which added more texture and also helped ground the bowl on the wooden tabletop. Last but not least, I added a fork and some chopsticks to the left of the bowl (**Figure 7.33**).

Figure 7.32
I changed the tabletop to a cool, textured surface, switched out the wooden bowl, and found a combination that worked much better for this scene.

Canon 5D Mark III · ISO 100 · 0.3 sec. · ƒ/5.6 · Canon 100mm ƒ/2.8L Macro lens

Figure 7.33
I finished off the props by adding cheesecloth under the bowl, a utensil to the left, and some small wooden items in the upper-left portion of the frame.

Canon 5D Mark III · ISO 100 · 0.7 sec. · ƒ/5.6 · Canon 100mm ƒ/2.8L Macro lens

In terms of styling and photography, soup can be a challenge. The soup is inside of a bowl, so the only area of the food that is visible is what you can see on the surface. Thankfully, this dish had a lot of elements that could easily be piled up high, so I had that in my favor. After I set my props up, I cooked and prepared the food using a recipe I received from a friend. Then, I filled the bowl with the soup broth and chicken and placed it on the set.

At first, the chicken pieces were bunched and pointing in odd directions (**Figure 7.34**). Ironically, the chicken does not actually show up in the final frame, but I still wanted it to be somewhat centered so that it did not mess with any of the garnish I knew I would be adding. The chicken also helped serve as a solid base to keep the garnish from sinking to the bottom of the bowl. So, using wooden chopsticks, I rearranged the chicken so that it was a little bit better for this setup (**Figure 7.35**).

Figure 7.34
When I first added the broth and meat to the bowl, the pieces of chicken were sticking out in odd directions.

Canon 5D Mark III · ISO 100 · 3 sec. · ƒ/5.6 · Canon 100mm ƒ/2.8L Macro lens

Figure 7.35
I used chopsticks to reposition the chicken so that it served as a better base for the garnish.

Canon 5D Mark III · ISO 100 · 4 sec. · ƒ/5.6 · Canon 100mm ƒ/2.8L Macro lens

Next it was time to add the garnish. If you are familiar with Khao Soi, you may have already noticed that my dish does not feature the traditional garnish of crispy fried noodles. Instead, I decided to use a pile of microgreens to add some color and also to make the dish healthier (after all, I will oftentimes eat the food after it is photographed). I made sure to pile them high up, and I also added some sautéed onions and a lime wedge in the background to diversify the colors in the scene (**Figure 7.36**).

Note

If you would like the recipe used with this dish, please visit http://foodbook.nicolesy.com.

Figure 7.36
To make the food more bright and colorful, I garnished it with microgreens, sautéed onions, and a lime wedge.

Canon 5D Mark III · ISO 400 · 6 sec. · ƒ/5.6 · Canon 100mm ƒ/2.8L Macro lens

Lighting Setup

The setup for this dish was simple sidelighting with the window to the right of the food. I used a large, 4'6" diffuser to soften the window light, and I also used a reflector to the right of the food for some of the shots. I did find that in most cases I preferred the images with more shadow one the left side of the food (**Figures 7.37** through **7.39**). An image with too much reflected light tends to make the food look flat, whereas the shadows on the bowl and food add depth to the scene.

Figure 7.37
For this image, I did not use any reflection on the left side of the food. Doing this helps give shadows and depth to the entire scene.

Canon 5D Mark III · ISO 400 · 6 sec. · f/5.6 · Canon 100mm f/2.8L Macro lens

Figure 7.38
I used a silver reflector to bounce light back into the left side of the frame. Notice how the amount of light makes the image look somewhat flat in comparison with Figure 7.37.

Canon 5D Mark III •
ISO 400 • 8 sec. •
f/5.6 • Canon 100mm
f/2.8L Macro lens

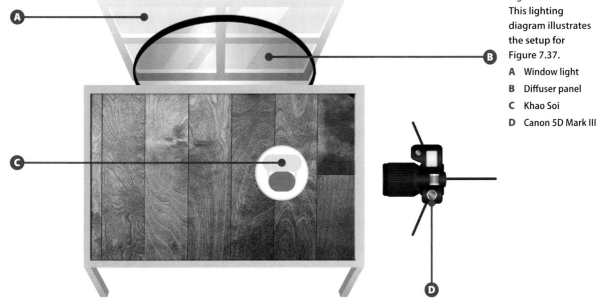

Figure 7.39
This lighting diagram illustrates the setup for Figure 7.37.

A Window light
B Diffuser panel
C Khao Soi
D Canon 5D Mark III

Postprocessing

Now let's go through the steps to process this photo in Lightroom.

Step 1: Open the Image in the Lightroom Develop Module

First, I select the photo and click the keyboard shortcut D to open it up into the Lightroom Develop module.

Step 2: Adjust the Tone Settings

In the Basic panel, I start by adjusting the tones (the white balance is accurate out of the camera, so there is no need to adjust it). First, I click the Auto button to see what it does. The Auto setting made the image a little too bright, so I decrease Highlights to –47 and Whites to –53. Then, I increase Contrast to +39 to make the image less flat.

Step 3: Adjust the Presence Settings

Next, in the Presence section, I increase Clarity to +23 to add some "crispness" to the image. I also increase Vibrance to +23 and Saturation to +14 to intensify and brighten up the colors.

Step 4: Increase Contrast with the Tone Curve

Now, in the Tone Curve panel, I select Strong Contrast from the Point Curve drop-down. I also decrease Highlights to –29 and increase Shadows to +44 to balance it and make the setting less dramatic.

Step 5: Add a Vignette

In the last step, I want to add a subtle vignette to darken the edges. So, I go to the Effects panel and direct my attention to the Post-Crop Vignetting section. Then, I set Amount to −15, Midpoint to 35, Roundness to +22, and Feather to +87.

Conclusion

When we are cooking, eating, serving, or just near food, there are a lot of senses at play. Not only can we see the food, we can also smell, taste, touch, feel, and even hear it. A heaping plate of something may not look appealing but can smell and taste so delicious that its looks don't matter. But when *only* looking at food, we have only our sense of sight to rely on. As photographers, it's our job to stimulate all of the senses with one photograph and make the food look as good as (or better than) it tastes.

Although this is a technical, "how to" book on food photography, there is a lot more to photography than gear and technique. If you're reading this book, especially if you've gotten this far, then you no doubt love food and are passionate about sharing that love with others through your photographs. Stay true to that love, let your passion drive you, and rely on your eyes to see light, colors, and textures. In other words, don't let your camera do all of the thinking for you.

It's also important to understand that you will never, ever finish the learning process as a photographer. It's so crucial to continually challenge yourself, test your limits, and try new things. Find a style of learning that works for you—whether it's reading books (like this one), watching videos, hands-on doing, or doing a bunch of research online. The key is to keep on growing and always move forward. Look at lots (and lots and lots) of beautiful food photographs and study *why* you like them. Photographers aren't photographers only when holding a camera; we are constantly (and oftentimes subconsciously) searching for our next photograph. So, try to *see* light even when you don't have your camera—watch how it falls across objects, creates shadows, and changes colors during the different parts of the day.

The bottom line is that making beautiful photographs of food is what we ultimately set out to do as food photographers, and I truly hope that this book is helpful to you in your journey. And don't forget that one of the biggest compliments you could ever receive about a food photograph is that it makes people hungry. When people want to eat something because they saw it in your image, then you're on the right track.

So stay hungry, find and create beautiful light, keep cooking, and always keep a camera close by—you never know when you'll find something beautiful.

Index

Numbers

35mm (and less) lenses. *see* Wide-angle lenses
35mm to 80mm lenses. *see* Midrange lenses
80mm (and greater) lenses. *see* Telephoto lenses
500px website, for portfolio setup, 129

A

Accessories. *see also* Props; Styling
    locating, 88
    using, 86–88
ACR (Adobe Camera Raw), for photo-editing, 153
Add command, for importing files, 161
Adobe Bridge, for photo-editing, 153
Adobe Camera Raw (ACR), for photo-editing, 153
Adobe Lightroom
    adding copyright to image metadata, 135
    alternatives for photo-editing, 153
    Basic panel editing options, 173–176
    calibrating monitor, 152, 180–181
    challenges in working with, 193
    collections for sorting/grouping photos,
        163–164
    creating catalogs, 154
    cropping/cloning photos, 171–172
    customizing panel views, 168
    Detail panel, 178–179
    Development Module, 149–151
    Effects panel, 180
    export presets, 191–192
    Export window, 187–191
    filtering selections, 170
    flags, color labels, and star ratings, 165–166
    folder organization, 162
    HSL panel, 177
    image processing with, 23, 147
    importing files already on computer, 161
    importing files from memory cards,
        155–160
    Lens Correction, 178–179
    Library Module, 148–149
    preparing files for export, 186
    presets, 183–185
    Split Toning panel, 178
    spot removal, 172–173
    Survey mode in photo selection, 169
        syncing settings between files, 182
        Tone Curve panel, 176
        view options in Library module, 167
        watermarks, 136
        working in, 153
Adobe Photoshop
    Digimarc Guardian plug-in, 140–141
    image processing with, 153
    watermarks, 136
Adobe Photoshop Elements, 140–141
Advertising
    ethical considerations in styling food, 66
    styled food vs. real food, 67–68
AlienBees B800 strobe light, 44–45
Aperture
    for blurred background, 99
    in calculating overall exposure, 32–33
    depth of field and, 29
    experimenting with depth of field, 35, 220
    focus and, 112
    intensity of light and, 50
    large aperture for blurred background, 41
    lens compression and, 110–112
    limitations of P&S cameras, 8–9
    midrange lens for blurred background, 16
    overview of, 27
    telephoto extender impacting, 17
Aperture Priority mode, factors in choosing, 33
Appetizer example
    adding a gradient, 213
    adjusting contrast, 212
    example photograph, 5
    focus point in, 202
    intensifying colors, 211
    lighting setup, 207–209
    overview of, 201
    photograph for book cover, 203
    postprocessing in Development module, 209
    props and styling, 204–207
    tone settings, 210
Apply During Import panel, 159
Artificial light
    intensity of, 50
    overview of, 42
    setup for, 44
    types of strobe lights, 45–46
Aspect ratio, cropping photos and, 171–172
Asymmetry, in composition, 100
Auto adjustments
    tone settings in grapefruit salad
        example, 236
    tone settings in green smoothie
        example, 223
    tone settings in Khao Soi example, 249
    of white balance, 25–26
AWB (auto white balance), in photographing
    food, 26

B

Backgrounds
    adding depth and messiness to, 196
    adding depth to composition, 81
    adding detail to balance composition, 62
    appetizer example, 207
    comparing wide lens with normal lens, 35
    in composition, 101–102
    lens compression and, 110
    midrange lenses and, 16
    not competing or interfering with main
        subject, 7
    positioning items in, 102
    soft. *see* Blurred (soft) background
    telephoto lenses and, 18
    wide-angle lenses and, 15
Backlight
    adding texture and depth to images, 51
    appetizer example, 207–208
    comparing with frontlight and sidelight, 58
    grapefruit salad example, 199, 232
    reflector use for, 46
    setup for, 52
    vinyl backdrop and, 92
Balance, in composition
    adding elements to balance scene, 62
    empty space in creating, 123
    minimalism and, 125
    overview of, 5–6
    Rule of Thirds, 100
    triangles and groups of threes, 102–103
Balance, white. *see* White balance
Ball heads, tripods, 21
Basic panel, Lightroom Development module
    editing options, 173–176
    overview of, 150
    tone settings in appetizer example, 210–211
    tone settings in grapefruit salad example, 235
    tone settings in green smoothie example, 222
    tone settings in Khao Soi example, 249
Batch processing, in Development module, 193
Battery use, Live View mode and, 74
Blogger.com, 126
Blogs
    controlling/maintaining, 131
    food blogger vs. food stylist, 66
    food blogging conferences, 133
    protecting digital content, 134
    protecting your blog, 141–143
    resources page on author's site, 145
    setting up, 126–128
Blur
    adding blur effect to photograph, 20
    depth of field and, 29
    slow shutter speed creating blur effect,
        28, 35

Blurred (soft) background
    aperture settings and, 99
    cupcake example, 41
    experimenting with depth of field, 35
    green mango smoothie example, 220
    large aperture for, 41
    lens compression and, 112
    midrange lenses and, 16
    telephoto lenses and, 18
    wide-angle lenses and, 15
Book cover, balancing photo and text on, 203
Bowls. *see* Dishes
Brackets, for tripod head, 22
Breadcrumb bar, Lightroom, 148, 150
Brightness
    adding to composition, 7
    gradients of, 213
    tone settings in appetizer example, 210
    tone settings in grapefruit salad example, 236
    tone settings in green smoothie example, 223

C

Cable releases
    equipment, 22
    using with tripod, 22
Calibration, of monitors, 152, 180–181
Camera Calibration panel, Lightroom
        Development module
    overview of, 150
    selecting process version, 180
    selecting process version and color profile,
        180–181
Camera mode, selecting, 33–34
Camera stands. *see* Tripods
CAN-SPAM Act of 2003, 132
Card readers, importing files from memory
        cards, 155
Catalog
    creating, 154
    folder organization in, 162
    importing files into, 155–161, 193
    installing downloaded presets, 184
    selecting/rating photos in, 165–166
Catalog panel, Adobe Lightroom Library
        Module, 148
Cheesecloth. *see* Fabrics
Chromatic aberration, correcting, 178–179
Clarity slider, adjusting Presence settings,
        175–176, 250
Cloning, spot removal and, 172–173
Close-ups, using macro lenses for, 17, 19
Cloudy, white balance settings, 24–26
Collection sets, 164
Collections panel
    creating collections, 163
    Development module, 150

Library module, 148
    types of collections, 164
Color labels
    filtering with, 170
    in photo selection, 166
Color section, Lens Correction panel, 179
Color wheels, 117–118
Colors
    adding to composition, 7, 117–118
    adjusting luminosity of, 238
    aesthetic use of, 5
    Basic edits using HSL panel, 177
    calibrating monitors, 152, 180–181
    continuous light and, 46
    in dessert example, 6
    editing with Vibrance and Saturation
        sliders, 175–176
    experimenting with, 119
    in french toast example, 39
    garnishes adding, 79
    intensifying with Vibrance and Saturation
        sliders, 211, 224
    of lighting, 49–50
    in pancake example, 65
    reflector impacting, 46
    white balance and, 24
Comments panel, Lightroom Library module, 149
Complementary colors, in composition, 117–118
Composition
    adding brightness and color, 7
    adding depth, 81
    adding flair, 98
    adding movement, 82
    background and foreground in, 101–102
    balancing, 5–6, 62
    challenges in working with, 119
    cherry blossom garnish example, 99
    color in, 117–118
    cupcake example, 40–41
    of elements into vertical orientation, 204
    empty space balancing, 123
    eye-level perspective, 108
    focus and, 112–115
    galette example, 96–97
    importance of focal length, 110–112
    improving photos with strong
        compositional elements, 95
    iPhone camera and, 10
    Khao Soi example, 243
    lens compression and, 110
    lines and corners in, 115
    minimalism and balance in, 125
    of overhead shot, 108–109, 206
    Rule of Thirds, 100
    shapes in, 115–116
    stand-ins for styling foods, 72
    three-quarters angle views, 106–107

timing and layers in, 38
    triangles and groups of threes, 102–103
    tripod use and, 21
    vertical and horizontal frames, 104–106
Conferences, attending, 133
Continuous lights, types of strobe lights, 45–46
Contrast
    increasing with Tone curve, 251
    shadows adding, 51
    tone settings in appetizer example, 210, 212
    tone settings in grapefruit salad example, 237
    tone settings in Khao Soi example, 249
Convert Photos to DNG option, Lightroom
        Library Module, 156
Copy and paste
    LIghtroom Development module, 150
    protecting text from, 143
Copy as DNG, import options, 156
Copy command, importing files already existing
        on computer, 161
Copyrights
    adding copyright footer to blog posts, 142
    adding to files on import, 158
    balancing sharing with protection, 144
    registering, 134–135
    visible watermarks indicating, 137
Corners
    in composition, 115
    positioning flatware in corner of photo, 117
    positioning items in background, 102
Crop sensors
    benefits of DSLR and mirrorless cameras, 12
    vs. full-frame sensor, 12–14
Crop tool, in Lightroom Development module,
        171–172
Curried noodle dish, style example, 62–63
Custom Brackets, 22

D

Darks. *see also* Contrast
    adding gradients to modify, 213
    adjusting contrast with Tone curve, 212
Database, 154. *see also* Catalog
Daylight. *see also* Natural light
    color of lighting and, 49
    common use in photographing food, 26
    white balance settings, 24–25
Depth
    adding to composition, 51, 81
    adding without being overwhelming, 198
    berries in background adding, 196
    Khao Soi example, 246
    loss in frontlight example, 57
    sidelight adding, 53
    textures adding, 89–92, 205

Depth of field
aperture and, 27
benefits of DSLR and mirrorless cameras, 12
experimenting with, 35
focus and, 29, 112
getting proper exposure, 26
green mango smoothie example, 220
limitations of P&S cameras, 8–9
midrange lenses and, 16
wide-angle lenses and, 15
Destination settings, import options, 160
Detail panel, Lightroom
overview of, 150
sharpening or noise reduction with, 178–179
Development module, Lightroom
Basic panel editing options, 173–176
Camera Calibration panel, 180–181
cropping/cloning photos, 171–172
Detail panel, 178–179
Effects panel, 180
HSL panel, 177
Lens Correction panel, 178–179
overview of interface, 149–151
presets, 183–185
Split Toning panel, 178
spot removal, 172–173
syncing settings between files, 182
Tone Curve panel, 176
in workflow, 153
Diffusers
appetizer example, 207
in backlight setup, 52
diffusion panels, 47
distance of light source from subject and, 50–51
in frontlight setup, 57
grapefruit salad example, 233
green mango smoothie example, 218
Khao Soi example, 246–247
modifying intensity of light, 50
in sidelight setup, 53–55
softboxes and umbrellas, 48
strobe lights and, 45
using diffusion panel with natural light, 43
Diffusion panels
in backlight setup, 52
in frontlight setup, 57
overview of, 47
in sidelight setup, 53–55
using with natural light, 43
Digimarc Guardian, for creating digital watermarks, 140–141
Digital cameras
determining which to buy, 14
DSLR and mirrorless, 11–12
full-frame sensor vs. crop sensor, 12–14
overview of, 8
P&S (point-and-shoot), 8–10

Digital content protection
balancing protection with sharing, 144
overview of, 134
protecting your blog, 141–143
registering copyrights, 134–135
using digital watermarks, 140–141
using visible watermarks, 136–139
Digital files. *see also* Files
overview of, 23
RAW vs. JPEG, 23–24
white balance and, 24–26
Direct marketing, building a mailing list, 131
Direction, of lighting
backlight, 51–52, 58
frontlight, 56–58
overview of, 51
sidelight, 53–55, 58
Dishes
adding bulk to shot, 76–77, 93
benefit of circular shapes, 116
color use and, 118
creating "rustic" feeling, 122
framing in overhead view, 124–125
in Khao Soi example, 242–243
positioning in composition, 204
props and styling for appetizer example, 205
props and styling for grapefruit salad, 227
relevance and simplicity in styling, 85
selecting for styling, 86–88
styling food with, 71
three-quarters angle view of contents, 107
Distance, of light source from subject, 50–51
Distortion
correcting in Lightroom, 178–179
lens compression and, 110
midrange lenses and, 16
wide-angle lenses and, 15
DNG files
export file settings, 188
import options, 156
what they are, 157
Domain name, setting up website and, 127
Downloads
installing downloaded presets, 184
resources page on author's site, 145
DSLR cameras, 11–12

E

E-books, copyrighting, 144
Editing. *see also* Adobe Lightroom
Basic panel options, 173–176
benefits of RAW file format, 23–24
Effects panel, Lightroom Development module
adding vignette to green smoothie example, 225
adding vignettes and film grain, 180
overview of, 150

Email, direct marketing via, 131
Environment, maintaining cleanliness of, 74–75, 216
Equipment. *see also* Digital cameras; Lenses
cable releases, 22
DSLR and mirrorless cameras, 11–12
full-frame sensors vs. crop sensors, 12–14
Lensbaby Composer Pro, 20
macro lenses, 17, 19
midrange lenses, 16
P&S (point-and-shoot) cameras, 8–10
purchase decisions, 14
telephoto lenses, 17–18
tripods, 21–22
wide-angle lenses, 15
Ergonomics, types of tripod heads and, 22
Ethical considerations
styled food vs. real food, 67–68
in styling food, 66
Export, Lightroom
Export button, 148
Export window, 187–191
preparing files for export, 186
presets, 191–192
for web use, 193
in workflow, 153
Exposure
adding a gradient to grapefruit salad example, 239
aperture and, 27
benefits of DSLR and mirrorless cameras, 12
calculating overall, 32–33
depth of field and, 29
determining which camera mode to use, 33–34
exposure triangle, 26
ISO, 30–32
limitations of P&S cameras, 8
shutter speed, 27–28, 30
tone settings in appetizer example, 210
Exposure triangle
calculating overall exposure, 32–33
overview of, 26
Eye-level perspective, in composition, 108

F

Fabrics
adding realism to style, 89–90
props and styling for appetizer example, 205
props and styling for grapefruit salad, 227
props and styling for green mango smoothie, 197, 215
props and styling for Khao Soi example, 243
Facebook, building a social media presence, 130
Farmer's market, ensuring food quality when styling food, 70

Fast lenses, aperture and, 27
File Handling panel, Lightroom import options, 159
File Renaming panel, Lightroom import options, 159
Files
    digital, 23–26
    export options in Lightroom, 187–191
    export presets in Lightroom, 191–192
    importing files already existing on computer, 161
    importing files from memory cards, 155–160
    organizing. see Organization/sorting
    preparing for export, 186
    pros/cons of deleting rejected photos, 170
    selecting/rating. see Selection, of photos
    storing in catalog, 154
    syncing settings between, 182
Fill lights, 46
Filmstrip
    Lightroom Development module, 150
    Lightroom Library module, 148
Filter controls
    Lightroom Development module, 150
    Lightroom Library module, 149
Filtering, in photo selection, 170
Flags
    creating smart collections of flagged photos, 164
    filtering selections by flag status, 170
    in photo selection, 165
Flashes
    Live View mode and, 74
    softboxes and umbrellas and, 48
    types of strobe lights, 45
    white balance settings, 25
Flatware. see Utensils
Flickr, website options for setting up portfolio, 129
Fluorescent light
    color balance and, 46
    quality of light, 48
    white balance and, 24–25
Focal length
    full-frame sensors vs. crop sensors, 14
    in iPhone examples, 10
    lens compression and, 110–112
    limitations of P&S cameras, 8
    macro, 17, 19
    midrange, 16
    overview of, 15
    prime and zoom lenses and, 17
    sensor type impacting, 13
    settings for natural light, 42
    shutter speed and, 30
    telephoto, 17–18
    wide-angle, 14–15

Focus point. see also Depth of field
    adjusting for text, 201–203
    appetizer example, 202
    benefits of DSLR and mirrorless cameras, 12
    depth of field and, 29
    finding best, 113–114
    garnishes creating, 79
    overview of, 112
    Rule of Thirds and, 100
    tips and tricks, 115
Folders
    installing downloaded presets in, 184
    organizing image files in, 162
Folders panel, Lightroom Library module, 148
Food stylists, benefits of hiring, 66
Foodgawker, website options for setting up portfolio, 129
Foreground
    in composition, 101–102
    lens compression and, 110
Forks. see Utensils
Formats, file settings, 188
Framing
    bowls in overhead view, 124–125
    experimenting with perspective, 119
    grapefruit salad shot, 228
    green mango smoothie shot, 215
    vertical and horizontal frames, 104–106
Freshness of ingredients
    ensuring food quality when styling food, 69–70
    stand-ins and, 72–73
Frontlight
    comparing with backlight and sidelight, 58
    overview of, 56
    setup for, 57
F-stop, for setting aperture, 27
Full-frame sensors
    benefits of DSLR and mirrorless cameras, 12
    vs. crop sensor, 12–14

G
Gadgets, in styling, 71
Garnishes
    backlighting, 232
    blueberries examples, 123, 216–217
    cherry blossom example, 99
    color use and, 118
    finding best focus point and, 113
    gadgets and tools for styling food, 71
    grapefruit salad example, 198–199, 229–230
    Khao Soi example, 243–245
    styling with, 79
Glare, reducing by using sidelight, 218

Glasses
    props and styling for green mango smoothie, 215
    relevance and simplicity of props in styling, 85
Glasses (photographic). see Lenses
Gradients
    appetizer example, 213
    grapefruit salad example, 239
Graininess, adding effects, 180
Grapefruit salad example
    adding gradient, 239
    adjusting color luminosity, 238
    adjusting white balance, 235
    brightening image, 236
    increasing contrast, 237
    lighting setup, 232–233
    overview of, 227
    photos, 198–200
    postprocessing, 234
    props and styling, 227–231
Graters, gadgets and tools for styling food, 71
Gray card, tools for setting white balance, 26
Green mango smoothie example
    adding a vignette, 225
    adjusting white balance, 222
    brightening image, 223
    intensifying colors, 224
    lighting setup, 218–220
    overview of, 197
    postprocessing, 221
    props and styling, 215–217
    thumbnails, 214
Grid view, options for viewing images in Library module, 167
Groups of threes, in composition, 102–103

H
Hard drives, exporting to, 187
Highlights
    adding a gradients, 239
    adjusting contrasts, 212
    tone settings in appetizer example, 210
    tone settings in Khao Soi example, 249, 251
Histogram and Photo Information
    Lightroom Development module, 150
    Lightroom Library module, 149
History panel, Lightroom Development module, 150
Horizontal frames, in composition, 104–106
HSL (hue, saturation, luminance), Lightroom Development module
    adjusting color luminosity, 238
    basic edits with, 177
    overview of, 150

I

Ice, real vs. fake, 80–82
Image display area, Lightroom Development module, 150
Image processing. *see* Adobe Lightroom
Image quality
    comparing DSLR and mirrorless cameras, 11
    sensor type impacting, 13–14
    telephoto extender impacting, 17
Import, Lightroom
    files existing on computer, 161, 193
    files from memory card, 155–160, 193
    Import button, 148
    presets, 160
    in workflow, 153
Instagram, building a social media presence, 130
Intellectual property.
    see Digital content protection
Intensity, of lighting, 50
Internet/online presence
    building a mailing list, 131–133
    creating a social media presence, 130–131
    setting up portfolio, 128–129
    setting up your website and blog, 126–128
    setting yourself up for online success, 121
    sharing and networking, 129
    website as online home, 126
iPhone, benefits of mobile phone cameras, 10
ISO settings
    calculating overall exposure, 32–33
    examples, 31
    iPhone examples, 10
    for natural light, 42
    noise and, 30, 32
    sensitivity of camera sensor to light, 30

J

JPEG files
    adding watermarks to, 190
    export settings, 188
    vs. RAW, 23–24
    white balance settings, 26

K

Kelvin, measuring temperature of light in, 24
Keyboard shortcuts, applying sorting methods with, 165
Keyword panels, Lightroom Library module, 149
Keywords, adding to files on import, 158–159
Khao Soi example
    adding vignette, 252
    adjusting Presence settings, 250
    adjusting tone settings, 249
    increasing contrast, 251
    lighting setup, 246–247

overview of, 241
postprocessing, 248
props and styling, 242–245

L

Landscape photography
    quality of light and timing of, 48
    telephoto lenses in, 17
    wide-angle lenses in, 15
Lastolite Tri-Grip reflector
    appetizer example, 208
    grapefruit salad example, 233
    overview of, 46
Layers
    in composition, 38
    for creating sense of fullness, 77–78
    in dessert photograph, 6
LCD monitors. *see* Monitors, calibrating
Lens compression
    composition and, 110
    experimenting with, 119
    focal length and, 110–112
    midrange lens example, 16
Lens Correction panel, Lightroom Development module, 150, 178–179
Lensbaby Composer Pro, 20
Lenses
    ability to change in DSLR and mirrorless cameras, 12
    fast lenses, 27
    keeping over time, 14
    Lensbaby Composer Pro, 20
    macro, 17, 19
    midrange, 16
    overview of, 15
    relationship of focal length to shutter speed, 30
    settings for natural light, 42
    telephoto, 17–18
    wide-angle, 15
Library module, Lightroom
    Collections panel for sorting/grouping photos, 163–164
    creating catalog, 154
    customizing panel views, 168
    filtering selections, 170
    flags, color labels, and star ratings, 165–166
    folder organization, 162
    importing files already on computer, 161
    importing files from memory cards, 155–160
    overview of interface, 148–149
    Survey mode in photo selection, 169
    view options, 167
    in workflow, 153
Light meters, calculating overall exposure, 32–33

Lighting
    adjusting contrast, 212
    aperture controlling amount of light entering camera, 27
    Artificial light, 42, 44–45
    backlight, 51–52, 58
    challenges in working with, 59
    color of, 49–50
    diffusers, 47–48
    direction of, 51
    distance of light source from subject, 50–51
    frontlight, 56–58
    getting proper exposure, 26
    intensity of, 50
    limitations of mobile phone cameras, 10
    Live View mode and, 34
    modifiers, 46
    natural light, 42–44
    overview of, 37
    quality of, 48
    reflectors, 46–47
    setup for appetizer example, 207–209
    setup for grapefruit salad example, 232–233
    setup for green mango smoothie example, 218–220
    setup for Khao Soi example, 246–247
    shutter speed controlling amount of light entering camera, 27–28
    sidelight, 53–55, 58
    stand-ins for styling foods, 72
    temperature of light sources in Kelvin, 24
    tripod use and, 21
    types of, 42
Lines, in composition, 115
Live View mode
    factors in choosing camera modes, 34
    finding best focus point, 115
    styling from camera view, 74
Logo, as visible watermark, 136
Loupe view, options for viewing images in Library module, 167
Low light conditions, limitations of mobile phone cameras, 10
Luminance. *see also* HSL (hue, saturation, luminance), Lightroom Development module
    adjusting color luminosity in grapefruit salad example, 238
    basic edits using HSL panel, 177

M

Macro lenses
    examples of use, 19
    full-frame sensors vs. crop sensors, 13
    when to use, 17
Mailchimp, 131–132

Mailing list, building, 131–133
Manfrotto Magic Arm, 82–83
Manual mode, factors in choosing camera
  modes, 33
Marketing
  benefits of mobile phone cameras, 10
  building a mailing list, 131
Memory card, importing files from, 155–160
Messiness
  adding detail to composition, 40
  adds realism, 80, 93
  in background, 196
  green mango smoothie example, 216–217
Metadata
  adding copyright to, 135
  adding to exported image, 189
  adding to files on import, 158–159
Metadata panel, Lightroom Library module, 149
Midrange lenses
  comparing wide lens with, 35
  when to use, 16
Mirrorless cameras
  overview of, 11–12
  previewing final image in, 115
Misting food
  for fresh look, 216
  when styling, 71
Mixing tools, for styling food, 71
Mobile phone cameras, uses and limitations, 10
Modifiers
  diffusers. see Diffusers
  experimenting with, 59
  overview of, 46
  reflectors. see Reflectors
  strobe lights and, 45
Module Picker
  Lightroom Development module, 151
  Lightroom Library module, 149
Monitors, calibrating, 152, 180–181
Move command, for importing files, 161
Movement, in styling, 82–83

N
Names
  File Renaming panel, 159
  renaming files during export, 188
Napkins
  color use and, 118
  props and styling for appetizer example, 205
  props and styling for grapefruit salad, 228
  relevance and simplicity of props in
    styling, 85
  textiles for adding realism to style, 89
Natural light. see also Sunlight
  Aperture Priority mode and, 33
  intensity of light and, 50

Live View mode and, 34
  meter use and, 32
  overview of, 42
  setup for, 43
Nature photography, telephoto lens in, 17.
  see also Landscape photography
Navigator panel
  Lightroom Development module, 150
  Lightroom Library module, 148
Networking (social). see also Sharing/
    networking; Social media
  attending conferences, 133
  building a mailing list, 131–133
  sharing and, 129
Newsletters, building a mailing list, 131–132
Noodle dish, style example, 62–63
Noise
  high ISO settings and, 30–32
  reducing with Lightroom Detail panel,
    178–179
Nondestructive editing, benefits of RAW files,
  23–24

O
Online presence. see Internet/online presence
Opacity, adjusting cloned area, 173
Optics, Lensbaby Composer Pro and, 20
Organization/sorting
  Collections panel for sorting/grouping
    photos, 163–164
  exercise, 193
  flags, color labels, and star ratings, 165–166
  folders, 162
  in Lightroom workflow, 153
Overhead view
  balancing composition, 206
  blueberry example, 143
  in composition, 108–109
  featuring various items on table, 124–125
  galette example, 96–97
  lens compression and, 110–112
  positioning tripod for, 208
  showing shapes and textures in, 123
  soup example, 125

P
P&S (point-and-shoot) cameras
  limitations of, 8–9
  mobile phone cameras, 10
  overview of, 8
Paint overlay, adjusting vignette effect, 225
Pan heads, types of tripod heads, 21–22
Pancake, style example, 64–65
Panels, hiding/revealing in Lightroom, 168

Pan/tilt head, types of tripod heads, 22
Paper towels
  gadgets and tools for styling food, 71
  working with messy foods, 75, 216
Peelers, tools for styling food, 71
Perfect Photo Suite, using in combination with
  Lightroom, 153
Perspective
  experimenting with, 119
  eye-level, 108
  overhead view, 108–109
  three-quarters angle, 106–107
  using height in composition of photo, 64
  vertical and horizontal frames, 104–106
Photo-editing software, 153.
  see also Adobe Lightroom
Pick Flag status, creating smart collections, 164
Plates. see Dishes
PNG files, 190
Point Curve. see Tone curves
Portfolio, creating, 128–129
Portrait photography
  quality of light and timing of, 48
  telephoto lens in, 17
Post-Crop Vignetting
  adding vignette to green smoothie
    example, 225
  adding vignette to Khao Soi example, 252
Postprocessing
  during export, 191
  with Lightroom. see Adobe Lightroom
Postprocessing, appetizer example
  adding gradient, 213
  adjusting contrast, 212
  adjusting tone settings, 210
  intensifying colors, 211
  overview of, 209
Postprocessing, grapefruit salad example
  adding gradient, 239
  adjusting color luminosity, 238
  adjusting white balance, 235
  brightening image, 236
  increasing contrast, 237
  overview of, 234
Postprocessing, green mango smoothie
  example
  adding vignette, 225
  adjusting white balance, 222
  brightening image, 223
  intensifying colors, 224
  overview of, 221
Postprocessing, Khao Soi example
  adding vignette, 252
  adjusting Presence settings, 250
  adjusting tone settings, 249
  increasing contrast, 251
  overview of, 248

Prep bowls, gadgets and tools for styling food, 71
Presence sliders
    basic edits, 175–176
    Khao Soi example, 250
Presentation, art of, 61. *see also* Styling
Presets, Lightroom
    export, 191–192
    import, 160
    installing, 184
    overview of, 183
    Presets panel in Development Module, 150
    saving, 185
Preview
    applying sorting methods from Preview
        window, 165
    cropping photos and, 171–172
    import options, 159
    viewing image before/after edits, 174
Previous button, Lightroom Development
        module, 150
Prime lenses, fixed focal length of, 17
Processing photos. *see* Development module,
    Lightroom
ProPhoto RGB, 188
Props
    adding bulk, 76–77
    appetizer example, 204–207
    dishes and accessories, 86–88
    experimenting with, 93
    grapefruit salad example, 227–231
    green mango smoothie example, 215–217
    Khao Soi example, 242–245
    relevance and simplicity, 85
    stand-ins for styling foods, 72–73
    in styling, 84
    textiles and textures, 89–92
PSD files, 188
Publish Services panel, Lightroom Library
        module, 148
Published images, not mixing with unpublished
        in copyright registration, 134

Q

Quality. *see also* Image quality
    ensuring food quality when styling food, 69
    of lighting, 48
    sensor type impacting, 13–14
    types of tripod heads, 22
Quick Develop panel, Lightroom Library
        module, 149

R

Ramekins
    gadgets and tools for styling food, 71
    triangle shape in composition, 103

RAW files
    converting to DNG, 156
    DNG file as type of, 157
    vs. JPEG, 23–24
Realism
    adding to composition, 198
    messiness adding, 80, 93
    textures adding, 89–92
Reciprocal exposures, 33
Reflective umbrellas, 48
Reflectors
    appetizer example, 207–208
    with artificial light, 44
    in backlight setup, 52
    curried noodle example, 63
    experimenting with, 59
    in frontlight setup, 57
    grapefruit salad example, 233
    green mango smoothie example, 218–219
    Khao Soi example, 246–247
    Live View mode and, 34
    with natural light, 43
    overview of, 46–47
    in sidelight setup, 53–55
Rejected photos, pros/cons of deleting, 170
Relevance, of props in styling, 85
Reset button, Lightroom Development
        module, 150
Restaurant setting, using frontlight in, 56
Right-click and copy protection, 143
Rim-lights, 51–52
RSS Feeds
    adding copyright footer to blog posts, 144
    protecting your blog, 142
Rule of Thirds
    in composition, 100
    finding best focus point, 113

S

Salad example. *see* Grapefruit salad example
Saturation. *see also* HSL (hue, saturation,
        luminance), Lightroom Development
        module
    adjusting Presence settings, 250
    basic edits, 175–177
    comparing standard color profile with
        landscape color profile, 181
    intensifying colors in appetizer example, 211
Sauces, prep bowls and ramekins for holding, 71
Screens. *see* Monitors, calibrating
Scrim, modifying intensity of light, 50
Security. *see* Digital content protection
Selection, of photos
    filtering in, 170
    flags, color labels, and star ratings, 165–166
    Survey mode in, 169

Sensors
    benefits of DSLR and mirrorless cameras, 12
    calculating overall exposure, 33
    full-frame sensors vs. crop sensors, 12–14
    ISO settings and, 30
    limitations of P&S cameras, 8
    shutter speed and, 27
Shade, white balance settings, 25–26
Shadows
    adding contrast to photos, 51
    adjusting contrast, 212
    in composition, 246
    loss in frontlight example, 57
    sidelight adding, 53, 55
    tone setting in green smoothie example, 223
    tone settings in appetizer example, 210
    tone settings in grapefruit salad example, 236
    tone settings in Khao Soi example, 251
Shapes
    in composition, 115–116
    in overhead view, 123
Sharing/networking
    attending conferences, 133
    balancing protection with, 144
    building a mailing list, 131–133
    growing a social media presence, 130–131
    overview of, 129
    photo sharing sites, 129
    protecting your blog, 141–143
Sharpening
    adding to exported image, 189
    with Clarity slider, 175–176
    with Lightroom Detail panel, 178–179
Sharpness, impact of telephoto extender on, 17
Shoot-through umbrellas, 48
Shutter speed
    Artificial light and, 42
    calculating overall exposure, 32–33
    example using slow shutter speed, 28
    limitations of P&S cameras, 8
    measuring, 30
    motion blur effect with slow shutter
        speed, 35
    natural light and, 42
    overview of, 27
    strobe lights and, 50
    sync speed of strobe light and, 46
    tripod use and, 21
Sidebars, hiding/revealing in Lightroom, 168
Sidelight
    comparing with backlight and frontlight, 58
    curried noodle disk example, 63
    green mango smoothie example, 218
    Khao Soi example, 246–247
    overview of, 53
    setup for, 53–55
Silverware, selecting for styling, 86.
        see also Utensils

Simplicity, of props in styling, 85
Size
    adjusting cloned area, 173
    file size settings during export, 188–189
Smart collections, 164
Smart Previews, 159
SmugMug.com
    right-click protection, 143
    website options for setting up portfolio, 129
Snapshots panel, Lightroom Development
    module, 150
Social media. see also Networking (social)
    benefits of mobile phone cameras, 10
    cautions, 131
    creating a social media presence, 130–131
Soft backgrounds. see Blurred (soft) background
Softboxes
    distance of light source from subject and,
        50–51
    modifying intensity of light, 50
    overview of, 48
    in strobe setup, 44–45
Sorting. see Organization/sorting
Source panel, of Import window, 156
Spam, knowing rules regarding, 132
Split Toning panel, Lightroom Development
    module, 150, 178
Spoons, styling food and, 71. see also Utensils
Spot Removal tool, in Lightroom Development
    module, 172–173
Spritzing fruit, for fresh look, 216
Squarespace.com, website creation services,
    127–128
Stand-ins
    ensuring food quality when styling food, 72
    examples, 73
    grapefruit salad example, 232
Star ratings
    filtering selections, 170
    in photo selection, 166
Strobe lights. see also Artificial light
    benefits of, 42
    color of lighting and, 49
    intensity of light and, 50
    Live View mode and, 74
    setup for, 44
    sync speed, 46
    types of, 45–46
Studio lights
    intensity of light and, 50
    quality of light and, 48
    softboxes and umbrellas and, 48
    types of strobe lights, 45–46
Styling
    appetizer example, 204–207
    art of presentation, 61
    from camera view, 74
    challenges in working with, 93

curried noodle dish example, 62–63
dishes and accessories, 86–88
ethical considerations, 66
food quality and, 69–70
food stylists, 66
gadgets and tools in, 71
garnishes in, 79
grapefruit salad example, 227–231
green mango smoothie example, 215–217
Khao Soi example, 242–245
maintaining clean environment, 74–75
messiness adding realism, 80
movement use, 82–83
pancake example, 64–65
props in, 84
real ice vs. fade ice, 80–82
relevance and simplicity in, 85
setup for, 231
stand-ins, 72–73
styled food vs. real food, 67–68
textiles and textures, 89–92
tips and tricks, 76–78
Sunlight. see also Natural light
    benefits of, 42
    color of lighting and, 49
    distance of light source from subject and, 51
    intensity of light and, 50
    variable quality of, 48
Survey mode
    in photo selection, 169
    sorting/organizing images, 193
Symmetry, composition and, 100–101
Sync speed, strobe lights, 46
Syncing
    batch processing and, 193
    Lightroom Library module, 149
    settings between files, 182

T

Tablecloths, textiles for adding realism to style, 89
Tabletops
    props and styling for grapefruit salad, 227
    props and styling for Khao Soi example,
        242–243
    use of color and, 118
    wood textured, 91–92
Tastespotting, website options for setting up
    portfolio, 129
Telephoto extender, 17
Telephoto lenses
    overview of, 17–18
    when shutter speed necessitates use of
        tripod, 30
Temperature
    adjusting white balance, 173–174
    measuring in Kelvin, 24

white balance in grapefruit salad
    example, 235
white balance in green smoothie
    example, 222
Text
    adding text watermarks to images, 190
    adjusting focal point for book title, 201–203
    protecting using right-click and copy
        protection, 143
Textiles, in styling. see Fabrics
Textures
    adding depth and realism with, 89–92, 205
    adding to picture, 4
    backlights adding to image, 51–52
    in dessert example, 6
    in french toast example, 38
    layers for adding bulk, 78
    overhead view of, 123
    styling, 89–92
Three-quarters angle, in composition, 106–107
Thumbnails
    green mango smoothie example, 214
    selecting images for importing, 158
TIFF files, 188
Tilt-shift lenses, Lensbaby Composer Pro
    imitating, 20
Timing, in composition, 38
Tint, adjusting white balance, 173–174
Tone
    adjusting in appetizer example, 210
    adjusting in grapefruit salad example, 236
    adjusting in green smoothie example, 223
    adjusting in Khao Soi example, 249
    basic edits, 175–176
    split toning, 178
Tone curves
    adjusting contrast in appetizer example, 212
    adjusting contrast in grapefruit salad
        example, 237
    adjusting contrast in Khao Soi example, 251
    LIghtroom Tone Curve panel, 150, 176
Tool Strip, Lightroom Development module, 150
Toolbars
    Lightroom Development module, 150
    Lightroom Library module, 148
    toggling visibility of, 166
Tools, in styling, 71
Triangles, in composition, 102–103
Tri-Grip diffusers. see Lastolite Tri-Grip reflector
Tripod heads, 21–22
Tripods
    Live View mode and, 34
    manual focusing, 115
    natural light and, 42
    positioning for overhead shot, 208
    shutter speed and, 27, 30
    tripod heads, 21–22
    types of, 21

Tungsten light
        color balance and, 46
        color of lighting, 49
        quality of light, 48
        white balance settings, 24–25
Tutorials, resources page on author's site, 145
Tweezers, gadgets and tools for styling food, 71
Twitter, building a social media presence, 130

U

Umbrellas
        distance of light source from subject and,
                50–51
        modifying intensity of light, 50
        overview of, 48
URL, setting up website and, 127
U.S. Copyright Office, 134
USB card reader, 155
Utensils
        adding flair, 98
        adding realism to setup, 198
        appetizer example, 205–206
        color use and, 118
        experimenting with props, 93
        grapefruit salad example, 227–228
        Khao Soi example, 243
        locating, 88
        Manfrotto Magic Arm example, 83
        positioning, 117
        relevance and simplicity in styling, 85
        selecting for styling, 71, 86–88

V

Variety, adding interest to photograph, 5
Vertical frames
        in composition, 104–106
        fitting elements into, 204
Vibrance slider
        adjusting Presence settings in Khao Soi
                example, 250
        basic edits, 175–176
        intensifying colors in appetizer example, 211
        intensifying colors in green mango
                smoothie, 224

Video files, exporting, 188
Video heads, types of tripod heads, 21
View options, in Lightroom
        Grid view and Loupe view, 167
        hiding/revealing panels, 168
        Survey mode, 169
Vignettes
        adding effects, 180
        correcting in Lightroom, 178–179
        green mango smoothie example, 225
        Khao Soi example, 252

W

Warm light, quality of light, 48
Water, misting food when styling, 71, 216
Watermark Editor, 190
Watermarks
        adding to exported image, 190
        comparing visible with digital, 144
        digital, 140–141
        tacky and classy, 138–139
        visible, 136–139
Websites
        controlling/maintaining, 131
        link to author's site, 121
        as online home, 126
        promoting via newsletter, 132
        protecting your blog, 141
        resources page on author's site, 145
        setting up portfolio on, 128–129
        setting up your own, 126–128
White balance
        basic edits, 173–174
        benefits of RAW file format, 23–24
        color of lighting and, 49
        digital files and, 24–26
        grapefruit salad example, 235
        green mango smoothie example, 222
        Live View mode and, 34
White foam board
        appetizer example, 207–208
        in backlight setup, 52
        in frontlight setup, 57
        grapefruit salad example, 233
        natural light and, 43
        in sidelight setup, 53–55, 63

        in strobe setup, 44
        use as reflector, 47
Whites
        tone settings in appetizer example, 210
        tone settings in grapefruit salad example, 236
        tone settings in Khao Soi example, 249
Wide-angle lenses
        full-frame sensors vs. crop sensors, 14
        playing with depth of field, 220
        when to use in food photography, 15
Window light
        appetizer example, 207–209
        in backlight setup, 52
        for diffused natural light, 42–43
        diffusion panel used with, 47
        in frontlight setup, 57
        grapefruit salad example, 233
        green mango smoothie example, 218
        Khao Soi example, 246–247
        modifying intensity of light, 50
        not having competing light sources, 50
        in sidelight setup, 53–55
Wordpress.com, blog creation services, 126
Wordpress.org
        protecting your blog, 141
        website creation services, 126–127
WYSIWYG (what you see is what you get), 127

X

.XMP files, 157
X-Rite ColorMunki Display, 152

Y

YouTube, building a social media presence, 130

Z

Zoom lenses
        comparing lens types, 35
        range of focal lengths in, 17
Zooming
        finding best focus point and, 115
        using with Detail panel, 179
        using with Presence sliders, 176
        using with spot removal, 172